GROWING UP
AMERICAN

A Novel

RAFAEL POLO

ISBN 978-1-64471-474-4 (Paperback)
ISBN 978-1-64471-475-1 (Hardcover)
ISBN 978-1-64471-476-8 (Digital)

Covenant Books, Inc.
11661 Hwy 707
Murrells Inlet, SC 29576
www.covenantbooks.com

PART I

CHAPTER 1

The eleven-year-old boy sat on the left rear seat of the car. His aunt Gloria looked out the window from the front passenger seat. The driver—well, he had no clue who the driver was—listened to WADO, a Spanish-speaking radio station. His older cousin Randy sat to his right, his mouth pouring words like a spilling pitcher. There were four people inside the car. Four different worlds revolving around an uncertain future.

The boy was small for his age, tipping the scales at less than a hundred pounds. An adult Labrador retriever easily outweighed him. He was wearing an old hand-me-down gray winter coat that smelled of mothballs and a fake rabbit fur hat with earflaps. He had light-brown hair, which some people called "dirty blond," light-brown eyes that changed to a grayish color in the light, and a terrific tan. He always had a terrific tan, having lived his entire life in Cuba. He stared out the window, a loud voice in his brain telling him, "What is wrong with you? Get control of yourself."

The scenery was completely foreign to the one he had abandoned four days earlier. A scene composed of ice, snow, and smoke rising from the sidewalk. As they parked the car, he pondered over what his new life would be like.

Now, it was a short walk from the parking lot to the apartment. His Tropical shoes "were" no match for the cold and icy sidewalk. He felt the chill rising from the soles of his feet, which was sending a frigid wave throughout his body. It was already getting dark, even though it was only about four o'clock in the afternoon.

A large outer door opened to a second inner door that led to the interior of the tenement building. The eerie hallway illuminated by a single lightbulb hanging tenuously from an unconcealed wire. The stairs covered with cracks like an old man's face, its lament echoing throughout the hallway as the small army march to the apartment.

It was a small apartment: one bedroom, a kitchen, bathroom, living room, one window with a view of the cluttered roof, and a second one looking down at busy South Main Street. Several people he never seen before huddled about the apartment. When bedtime arrived, he asked his aunt:

"When are the strangers leaving?"

She told him they have nowhere to go. The strangers picked a spot on the cold linoleum and tried to go to sleep.

Marco arrived in mid-December. Christmas was right around the corner. The streets and businesses decorated with bright lights, just like pre-Castro Cuba. A large figure of Santa Claus riding a sled full of presents arched high over North Main Street flashing that Santa was on his way bringing joy to millions of kids. Marco hoped he would be one of the lucky ones.

Christmas Day arrived, and Marco was surprised to see presents under the tree bearing his name. His aunt and uncle bought him winter shoes and clothes. He appreciated his aunt and uncle's sacrifice. He never forgot that special day.

CHAPTER 2

There are forces at work around us, notorious like angry water bursting through a doomed dam, extinguishing everything and everyone in its path. Leaving only misery and despair in its wake.

Marco's world turned upside down on January 1, 1959. For nearly three years, a guerrilla war waged in the Sierra Maestra, the mountainous region in eastern Cuba's Oriente Province. Although the Castro forces were nearly wiped out when they made their initial landing on that rugged coast, he and his rebels managed to survive.

Every era has a superior sort of journalist. They call themselves "truth seekers" when, in fact, they get a hold of an idea and then alter it to fit their agenda. Herbert L. Matthews was such a journalist. In February 1957, as a reporter for the *New York Times* (NYT), he turned Fidel Castro into a revolutionary idol. In a *NYT* article, Matthews wrote that Castro was still alive and that he alone had seen him in his hideout in the rugged, almost impenetrable Sierra Maestra. Matthews's experience with revolutionary movements dated back to his work for the *NYT* during the Spanish Civil War (1936–1939). He was subjected to criticism for showing communist tendencies, a charge he later rejected.

As 1958 came to an end and 1959 began, Castro and his *barbudos*, the bearded men, defeated Batista's better equipped but corruptly lead army. The Castro forces, cautious in their victory march toward Havana, secured their flanks before entering the capital in the early days of 1959. In the meantime, Fulgencio Batista, the venal Cuban dictator, fled the country with his family and cronies while simultaneously carrying away a mountain of cash, jewels, and gold. He left behind supporters that now had no lifeline and were to live or die by their wits.

Marco's father, a master sergeant in Batista's air force, assigned to the paraloft department, was rounded up and imprisoned along with other military men. When his dad was finally released, he overheard a conversation between his parents. His dad's friend asked for water. The response—a bullet to the leg. Without medical assistance, the man bled out and died.

Marco lived with his parents on Avenida 13, Calle 86, Numero 8610, a two-bedroom, one bath, kitchen, living room, dining room house with a small garden. The home was located on a street, which ended next to Columbia Air Base. The constant drone of airplanes taking off and landing was routine fare in the neighborhood.

There was a pharmacy at the beginning of the dead-end street; it was also the bus stop for the Ruta 30 bus line. Across from the bus stop was a bodega. The bodega doubled as small restaurant. People went there for a quick meal and to play dominos. The constant talk and the crashing of dominos as the players move them in preparation for the next game provided a warm and friendly atmosphere in the neighborhood.

The jukebox played Cuban music that was known throughout the world and often copied. Ernesto Lecuona, a famed composer and renowned pianist, wrote many works incorporating Cuban rhythms and lyrics that are still famous to this day. The music of the Orquesta Aragon, La Sonora Matanzera with Celia Cruz, Perez Prado, and Beny Moret was popular in Europe, North and South America. Mambo, cha-cha-cha, and rumba are examples of Cuban dances still popular today.

A great Marxist storm cloud destroyed that warm neighborhood atmosphere. Of all forms of culture, the most uplifting is music. Music is vitalizing and popular because music reaches thousands at once. The Cuban government now turned to music as a form of indoctrination. The revolutionary radio stations forced the worker's Marxist anthem, "The Internationale," on the people incessantly playing over the airwaves without considering that taste cannot be crassly enforced because either it is innate, or it is not. It was a futile measure for educating the inchoate Cuban proletariat. Tropical, sensuous, sultry rhythms do not mix with cold, stoic marches.

It seemed that overnight "friends" now treated Marco and his family like vermin; they did not know it, but his family had entered Dante's Ninth Circle of Hell—Treachery. Under the new regime, there was no such thing as truth, at least not in the absolute sense, only revolutionary truth.

The state was now the supreme corporation that never dies. Castro's agitprop, at first, produced polls engineered to influence rather than assess the opinions of Cubans. This was the velvet approach; if it did not work to rile the population into rabid American hatred, he would use the hammer approach: jail and execution. One way or the other, he was going to get his false message across to the people. It was not long before friends and even families were spying on each other—all to gain favor with the new Cuban lord and maybe a sinecure. Citizens had no redress, for the new dictator controlled the three branches of government: the legislative, the executive, and the judicial.

His family could not understand the attraction to Marxism. It offered nothing and demanded everything, including your soul. It operated as the supreme autonomous corporation dedicated to manipulating the people for the benefit of party members.

The next couple of years saw his country transform from a military dictatorship to a totalitarian dictatorship. Private property was no longer recognized, farms collectivized. In short, all property belonged to the state.

The counterrevolutionaries fought back, but without success. The Castro police, like a pack of hungry lions, took down the agile anti-revolutionary cheetah. Many counterrevolutionaries were killed or capture. The lucky ones escaped to start new lives in foreign lands.

Not a single captive was shot without a trial. The scenario of this ghastly movie started and ended in the same pernicious way. The proceedings lasted a few minutes. The "prosecutor" nearly always demanded the death penalty, *Paredón*, a firing squad. The lucky ones were sentenced to thirty years of hard labor on Isla de Pinos, Cuba's penal colony. The same jail Castro and his brother Raul had spent time following their mad attempt at overthrowing Batista's government when they and a few of their early followers assaulted the Moncada army barracks on July 26, 1953. Except the brothers did not make big rocks into little ones; instead they were allowed to read books and enjoy family visits.

It was only a matter of time before Marxist indoctrination found its way into the school system. A school is much like a container, a vessel, into which children are deposited while young and fragile. Here, their minds were molded to follow good Marxist standards demanding an end to poverty and, most importantly, social justice. This was the opportunity to rewrite history in the Marxist model. Marxism will provide healthcare for all, commerce governed by the state and not private individuals, and the beautification of the communities by government diction instead of artists' concepts. It was all set.

People provided for people, it was so tangible one could touch the results—so pronounced the Marxist government leaders from their pulpits. A good Marxist is very much quite unthinkable as an honest thief. Secularism is the answer in the Marxist world. Religion is nothing more than a concept for the soul, if there is such thing as a soul. Live in the present reality and not in the bounds of the unknown. The problem was that the majority of Cubans were Catholics even though they often failed to follow their religion's tenets. There was still a fear of hell, even though they were afraid to admit it. The idea that God's scrutinizing eye still saw into the souls of the believers made the battle Marxists had to fight against Christianity that much harder. There was much work to be done in destroying centuries of old practices; with not one minute to lose, change started with the children's indoctrination.

The Marxists teacher and administrators in charge of the school system were under a solemn obligation. They were responsible for the beliefs on the new generations, in fact, the molders of public opinion. In other words, Marxist teachers are responsible for the thoughts of the coming generation, so you must catch them, teach them while they are young. The presumption being that they could create via state action the exact kind of human beings and social order that they wanted. The state must remove all external constraints—legal, economic, educational, and environmental—that hamper's society's fulfillment.

Marco's school Colegio Naredo was located about five blocks from his home in Marianao. Recently, the school received multiple visits from the *barbudos*. The Marxist's ideals of Che Guevara and Camilo Cienfuegos were hammered into the children's minds. Their pictures hung on the walls, looking down at the students, making everyone uncomfortable believing that someway, somehow, they eavesdrop on what was being said.

When he told his parents about the barbudos visits, he completed the semester, but was not matriculated for the next one. He would not see the inside of a classroom again until his first day of school in America six months later.

CHAPTER 3

First day of school. Turned right on 15 South Main Street, eyes locked on every structure like a fire control radar on a target. Turned left by the furniture store and crossed the street. On the left a stationary store. Men talking and smoking looked like they might be waiting for someone or something. His aunt leading the way. Up Westchester Avenue, passed more men talking and smoking in front of a convenience store. Walked under the railroad trestle, a train slowing down as it reached its destination. A pizzeria on the left, not open. Crossed the street. On the right a variety of businesses, and on the left a beautiful church, its architecture different from the Roman Catholic churches he was used to seeing in Cuba. His head up and walking at a brisk pace. He always walked at a brisk pace. On the right a big fire station with opened doors displaying ruby-red fire engines. On the left more small stores and a bar. Crossed over a couple of more streets, and on his right a beautiful building, the post office, and next to it another impressive building, the public library. Turned left into Elm Street, and there it was his new school, Our Lady of Mercy (OLM).

Wearing his OLM uniform, white shirt, blue tie, and dark-blue pants, his aunt escorted him inside the school. She was waiting for them by the entrance, a tall nun with a countenance that said, "I'm the boss." Marco looked up to the school principal with respect and a bit of fear.

His aunt left for work, and the principal took him to meet his new fifth-grade classmates. The teacher, Mrs. Frey, a compassionate and gifted teacher, assisted Marco with his schoolwork. Marco spoke very little English and, for now, felt like a Martian around his new mates, a mixture of boys and girls totaling sixteen.

Pictures of the Virgin Mary and John F. Kennedy hung on the walls. A depiction of the Crucifixion centered above a large green chalkboard. An American flag was proudly displayed. Everything orderly and clean—perfect environment for learning. The school day started with prayer and the Pledge of Allegiance. In Cuba, the school day started with indoctrination on the virtues of Marxism and no prayers.

The days passed quickly by. Marco's was feeling confident in his new environment. He was making new friends, and language was no longer a problem as he swiftly became fluent in English. TV shows on WPIX, Channel 11, like *Officer Joe Bolton* and *Soupy Sales*, helped overcome the language barrier.

Sometimes after school, he would walk to Jimmy's house, his new school friend. Jimmy introduced him to his mom, dad, and five sisters. His oldest sister found Marco an interesting study. Here was this young boy who came to America to live with his aunt while his parents remained in Cuba and, after a couple of months, spoke English and adapted to the new culture like a bird takes to flight.

CHAPTER 4

Sitting at the kitchen table, Marco wrote to his parents in Cuba. In early 1962, correspondence between the countries was still possible. He let them know that everything was good and he was learning English and making friends.

He thought about Cuba and pictured the trip from his home in Marianao to his grandmother's apartment in Lawton. Pre-Castro public transportation in Havana was outstanding. Bus lines covered the entire city with clean, affordable, dependable transportation. A passenger seldom had to wait more than five minutes before a *guagua*, a bus, carried him to his destination.

Marco recalled how they would board the Ruta 30 guagua at the beginning of his street. The bus would make several stops at designated areas, picking up and discharging passengers on its way to Lawton. A favorite sight on the way to his grandma's place was the grand entrance to the Universidad de la Habana with its wide and majestic stairs. The university was founded in 1728, the oldest university in Cuba, and one of the oldest in the Americas.

He flashbacked to a time before Castro—a happy time. A Cuban Air Force bus would pick up military dependents and take them to the beach. His mom would prepare a *merienda*, a small lunch. The downside to having lunch was that his mom would not let him go in the water for a full three hours. The reason being an *embolia*. His mom's definition of an embolia was a sort of cramp that would stop the digestive process, prevent movement, and then, of course, drowning because embolia only happened in deep water.

Baseball is a sort of religion in Cuba. It seems that every newborn comes equipped with the baseball gene in his DNA. Marco's uncle took him to a night ballgame in Havana. When he saw the beautifully manicured infield and emerald green outfield, he thought he had just walked into heaven. The Havana Sugar Kings an International League, Triple A team affiliated with Major League Baseball's Cincinnati Reds was playing that night.

He remembered sitting with his mom on the *malecón*—a broad esplanade, roadway, and seawall—looking north at the blueish-green ocean horizon that seemed to go on forever. Sometimes the roaring surf smashed the seawall, sending salty sea spray high in the air, soaking the sidewalk as it came down, making puddles, and unleashing a wonderful rejuvenating scent that cleansed the soul from all that is evil.

He replayed these memories and others attempting to never forget his homeland, but like everything in life, time has a way of moving on. If you fail to keep up with the present, you fall behind. Marco, in his short life, was learning to live in the present. Memories of his motherland became more and more distant as time ticked by.

Marco spared himself from mental agony by viewing his new life with eyes half opened. Then events superseded, awakening him to the new circumstances and forcing him to open his eyes fully and accept his new environment.

Life with his aunt, uncle, and cousin was safe, but it was not the same as living with his parents. His aunt and uncle both worked in factories, and his older cousin was a student at Port Chester High School.

Marco was usually the first one back at the apartment. The strangers, by now, had found their own ways. He did his schoolwork and then watch TV. His cousin was usually the next person to arrive. Five years older than Marco and with a hair-trigger temper. His cousin Randy had always been a difficult character to deal with, even under ideal circumstances, but recently, he had become a Jehovah's Witness and liked to proselytize on his younger cousin.

Randy unsuccessfully tried to convert Marco from Catholicism to Jehovah's Witness. Time and again, Marco rebuffed his cousin's lectures, each time making Randy angrier and angrier. One day after school, Marco was listening to the radio. Randy came into the apartment and said he wanted to listen to a different station. Marco stood his ground as he was listening to music he liked. In a rage, Randy pulled the radio electrical wire from the socket and, in one spiteful motion, threw it on the floor with all his might. The radio shattered in "a million pieces," making a loud bang. Marco, dismayed with his cousin's behavior, wished he was back with his parents.

CHAPTER 5

Speculation was that the new Marxist government was planning to send minors to the Soviet Union to serve in work camps. Like nervous animals in a cage pacing back and forth, panicked Cuban families that could not afford to immigrate to the United States search for an escape from the Marxist cage. Then as if the heavens had answered thousands of prayers, a new opportunity for unaccompanied minors to travel to Miami became a reality.

Until early in 1962, children were required to have a visa and twenty-five dollars for airfare travel to the United States. In 1960, the Catholic Church in conjunction with the State Department created the Peter Pan Project. Unaccompanied children could now travel to the United States without the visa requirement. The children were relocated with family members already living in the US, sent to a Catholic orphanage, or resettled with an American family.

Over fourteen thousand unaccompanied Cuban minors made the ninety-mile trip to Miami between 1960 and 1962. Marco was one of the lucky ones to leave the imprisoned island.

It became visible as a firefly in the dark that the political climate was swiftly getting more and more oppressive. In mid-1960s, Marco sat on his father's lap. His dad, a big man, six foot tall, weighing two hundred pounds. There was tension in the air, like a cloud ready to burst following lightning and thunder. Marco had never seen his dad so serious. His father said it was time for Marco to make an adult decision. Marco was nine years old.

"Son, tonight, you have to make a tough choice, one that will follow you for the rest of your life. Either you stay here with us, or you travel to New York to live with your aunt. If you decide to go, you'll have the opportunity to take charge of your life. To make your own mistakes and to mend them if you have the moral courage. However, should you decide to go, there is a strong possibility that we will be separated for a long time, perhaps forever. Hopefully, Castro will be gone in short order and we'll be reunited here in Havana.

"Or you could stay here. This country is now a Marxist dictatorship. You have seen the vicious treatment we receive from our 'friends.' We no longer have the freedom to choose our way of life. Justice has been removed, and we are left with gangs of criminals. The Marxist collect and scatter lies. People desire the freedom to pursue happiness, but the latitude to chase that goal is also gone. The individual does not matter—what matters is the survival of the Communist Party. Now, it is up to you to decide—to go or to stay."

The bottom line was if he went, he may never see his parents again, and if he stayed, he would remain with his parents. He would go to New York. He knew this was the decision his parents wanted him to make.

Similar conversations were taking place throughout the island. The great Cuban diaspora was about to begin. They would leave everything they owned, their culture, their language, and embark on an unplanned voyage. Like a floundering ship in a storm at the mercy of the wind and currents taking it to destinations unknown. With them went much of the technical, agricultural, financial, and administrative expertise that Cuba would sorely need in the years ahead. Lawyers, doctors, architects, musicians, plumbers, and electricians made their way to the United States, Venezuela, Spain, Dominican Republic, and other foreign lands. The island was abandoned by the same professional class that helped oust the Batista government.

CHAPTER 6

Fact, not rhetoric! In communist Cuba, it was not important to be a productive member of society, whether you were an engineer, writer, medical doctor, or janitor. What really mattered was complete loyalty to the Communist Party. It was as if a member's loyalty lies first with the party and then, and only then, came Cuba's welfare. Once talking points were approved by the party, there was no deviation. They stuck together despite false, outlandish promises that could never be kept. Deviation meant that you would be identified as a traitor.

In a world where the walls have recording devices and your neighbor works for the secret police, conversation is safest while walking. Jealousy was commonplace as the victors lived for revenge. Scores were settled as Fidelistas, Castro followers, accused the *gusanos*, the anti-Castro people, on a variety of trumped-up charges. Eventually, the fictitious charges take root, your belongings stolen and redistributed.

There are also those who preach society to deny individualism. *El partido*, the party, is the heartbeat of the dictatorial power. Despite the Cuban leadership's failure in providing essential subsistence for the people, the party, without a good answer, lied instead and told them that in the near future, their standard of living would improve. In reality, the only part of the population living well were the party's high official. There were two sets of truth in the new communist system. One for the masses, for the population at large, and second set of truths for the party faithful, the chosen, the insider.

Within a short time, his old neighborhood lost its intimacy. Everyone's turned inward, guarding their secrets like a banker protects his money. From the decision for Marco's travel to New York came open hostility from former "friends." Name-calling—*esbirro* (minion) and *gusano* (worm)—became commonplace. People were stung with humiliation; inside them, angry voices kept telling them they were cowards, that they should make some hollow gesture of protest. Then reality hit—if you fought back, an uninvited official from the Comite de Defensa would knock on your door and make you wish you were never born.

The main responsibility of the jefe of the Comite de Defensa is to monitor all movement in the neighborhood. For example, the time someone left their house and returned, the person who visited their home, and if he had carried a bag or had a bag when he left. This sycophant reported to a higher authority.

The pattern was clear. "Friends" were making reports to the comite on a daily or weekly basis depending on how much "information" was collected. In other words, they deliver a few lives, maybe friends or acquaintances, to concoct cases. The idea was to pretend to be someone's "friend." Some thought they could escape prison by associating with the comite; in due time, some of them were also being taken to a cell under police escort.

If there was any doubt about your loyalty to the new revolutionary government, your travel plans could be derailed, and perhaps a reeducation period was in order to erase your misguided bourgeois ways.

The new leftist regime promised a classless society. However, just like in George Orwell's *Animal Farm*, in the new Cuban "farm," some people are more equal than others. By becoming an informer, the ladder to a better life and maybe even earning a promotion was available since it placed you on good terms with the ever-dangerous police that protected you while simultaneously using you.

Once this slippery slope way of life commenced, no friendships or loyalties can intervene to pull in the reins on you. You are now forced to advance, sliding further into deep well of corruption from where there is no recovery. These agents of influence now control public opinion and create a hate-filled atmosphere as they raise the people's already hot blood by repeatedly shouting slogans like, "Cuba si! Yankis no!"

They do not have any scruples, but try to present a human face. The deception continues until they have total and complete power. It was too late then to realize that a Marxist is committed to sure cures that always turn out to be palliative measures—no, better yet, swindles.

The end game is that everyone is suspicious of everyone. If labeled a "counterrevolutionary"—and that could entail anything from telling a joke about Fidel to being associated with someone fallen out of favor—even an innocent child's remark could bring down an avalanche of pain.

Marxists want what capitalists have, but they don't want to earn it; instead, they take it by subterfuge or force. On one hand, Marxists harangue about the plight of the less fortunate, the downtrodden. They feel their pain, in words, not deeds, and resort to improving their dismal lives by providing the bear minimum, as if that satisfies all men's souls: an apartment in a tenement, a stipend to buy food, and a minimum of health care—God forbid you have a serious ailment.

On the other hand, Marxist elite never wear hand-me-down clothes. They are dressed in the finest garments available. Cuban Party members moved into the most luxurious home in Varadero and Miramar, exclusive neighborhoods. The same neighborhood where Bacardi—yes, the very same world-famous rum maker—resided with his family. The party elite did not move into the neighborhoods of the masses to live alongside the people they championed.

CHAPTER 7

The barbudos systematically rounded up all law enforcement officials, judges, and merchants, and all faced an uncertain fate. Thousands were tried as "counterrevolutionaries" or disappeared into the hands of hastily arranged show trials, and sadly, the crowds condoned the vengeance of the victors. In many areas, the revolutionaries' actions encouraged communal fears and jealousies, mob violence, and acts of revenge and retaliation.

Marco's mom took him to the western province of Pinar del Rio, where his uncle, his mom's brother, was incarcerated. His uncle was a successful businessman who had been accused of corruption by a competitor. His cousin, his uncle's daughter, drove Marco and his mom to the jail in her jeep.

There was total confusion at the jailer's desk. The chief jailer, a peasant with a pockmarked face resembling a crunched paper bag, the arbiter of all cases, with the self-assurance of an untouchable, rubbed his jaw as if nursing a toothache. Behind him a picture of a smiling Fidel Castro with his ubiquitous cigar overseeing the proceedings.

He found the odor sickening, inescapable, his eyes watering from the powerful smell of the soiled, scared men. His uncle was occupying a small cell, normally occupied by the town drunk. The prisoners were stacked in the claustrophobic calaboose like sardines in a tin can—no room to sit or lay. His uncle's expression was one of dejection, as if death was calling, and he was incapable of rejecting its invitation.

His mom had a brief exchange with his uncle, as visiting time was short. She managed to raise his spirits. Sometime later, his uncle was released from prison after many people came to his defense citing that he was an honorable man.

Then his cousin took him and his mom to a nearby cemetery where a number of antirevolutionaries had recently been shot and buried. They reached the cemetery as the sun was going down and the skies turning overcast. They walked on soggy ground, observing the newly dug graves. There was a rumor that the ghosts of the recently shot had been wandering the grounds. Although Cuba was heavily Catholic, there was also lots of superstitious beliefs.

One grave in particular was readied with little sympathy for the dead man. It turned out that this was the grave they came to visit. He was Juan Guerra, an antirevolutionary that did not easily surrendered to the Castro thugs. Instead, he fought and took out several of his persecutors. He used the last bullet to kill himself rather than surrendering. He was buried in a shallow grave, part of his casket exposed to the elements.

Then it became eerily quiet, as if the heavens had said you have seen enough. No sound, except for that of a moist breeze that whipped leaves in a circular motion. Suddenly, the wind picked up in ferocity, and rain pelted down in warm, heavy drops. It was time to go, and he was glad. He left behind a depressing and noisome day.

CHAPTER 8

The rapacious hand of power seizes upon everything. Marco was walking with his father and his father's friend. The friend said that "he doesn't understand why people have to stand in line to buy food. Why do people have a rationing book that you can only buy a couple of items at a time? Cuba's land is fertile, all you have to do is throw a seed on the ground, and it will grow. I don't understand what is happening to our country."

"The answer to the shortages of food was easy to trace," said his Dad. "It is collectivization!" Under Marxism, misery is the only real opportunity.

All landowners now fell under the same category, the *latifundistas*. In the recent past, this term was reserved for large landowners; now it referred to anyone that owned even a small tract of land. Stalin turned private farms into collective ones in the Soviet Union. The *kulaks*, private landowners, were deemed enemies of the state by the Marxist regime. The result of collectivization was the death of millions of people due to starvation and famine. Latifundistas were also regarded as enemies of the new Cuban regime. The failed system was tried in Cuba, and it also failed just as it did in the Soviet Union some thirty years earlier.

Each and every day under Marxism, the people had less liberty. Instead of improving the people's well-being, the failing system created shortages of nearly everything. The result was the emergence of a black market. There you could buy almost anything if you knew key people and had real money to spend.

God has forgotten us. Desperate people often find consolation in divine power. So was the case sometime in the 1960s or early 1961. Early one morning, a family saw an image of the Virgin Mary nestling on a mountain. The apparition reappeared numerous times over the following weeks. The rumor, as it often is the case, spread like wildfire throughout the area and finally reached Havana.

Early one morning, Marco and his mom piled onboard a neighbor's 1958 blue Plymouth for the two-hour ride to view Divine Providence. Driving west, Marco marveled at the beautiful scenery before him. Verdant scenery framed the entire horizon, royal palm trees that thickened in the distance while reaching to the sky, and decorous mountains blanketed the landscape, and above it all, a blue sky dotted with puffy clouds that resembled cotton balls making the drive to their destination, El Valle de Viñales, hopeful and peaceful.

Apparently, Virgin Mary, only appeared early in the morning, bringing her message that relief from Marxist bondage was on its way. They arrived at the site to find dozens of vehicles filled with the faithful: oxen-drawn carts, buses, and cars. On this day, to everyone's disappointment, Mary did not appear, but it turned out to be an educational outing for Marco anyway. He got to see beautiful scenery. On the way home, he listened to adult conversation regarding politics and religion. The only subject missing was sex.

No sooner they had returned to *Marianao* than there were whispers that free Cubans backed by Americans were going to invade the island. Could it be that the Virgin Mary was working on that miracle? The anti-Fidelistas sensed victory. Of this they were absolutely sure because the United States never backed a loser. It was going to happen the Castro regime was on its last leg. With heavenly assistance and the military and financial power of the United States, no failure was in sight.

It all changed in April 1961. Until that time, the United States had never lost a war, above all, had never abandoned a friend. The dawn's stillness was broken by the roar of a low-flying airplane. On 15 April 1961, a vintage World War II B-26 twin-engine light bomber ripped the air base with bombs and machine-gun fire. Columbia Air Base was under attack by the free Cubans.

His mother yelled for him to take shelter in her bedroom. His mom had a large statute of San Lazaro, reverently displayed on corner of the bedroom. The ground shook from the violence. His Mom, seeking divine protection for her son, told him to get under the statute. He resisted the idea. He thought that with the raid's fierceness, San Lazaro could fall from his lofty perch and bonk him on the head. Instead, he moved to a safer location.

The lone B-26 picked up speed and banked into its attack profile, this time hitting an ammunition dump before leaving in its wake high plumes of smoke and secondary explosions. Experts write that the art of warfare at all levels is to obtain and maintain freedom of action while denying it to the enemy. That is the ability to carry out critically important, multiple, and diverse decisions to accomplish assigned military objectives. Certainly, with the first attack wave completed, more waves, designed to destroy Castro's air force on the ground, would follow. However, this never materialized. That attack was the only one on Castro's main air base. Castro's air wing was intact and ready to repel the invading flotilla when it reached Cuban shores.

US politics trumped over the success of the invasion and the lives of the invaders. The Kennedy administration canceled the follow-on airstrikes. The neutered Bay of Pigs plan was completed in the late afternoon of 16 April 1961. No airstrikes by the brigade air force would be permitted until they could originate from airfields in Cuba. From now on, the brigade air force would be restricted to missions of "tactical necessity" and only over the beachhead. "Tactical necessity," diplomatic words by armed chair tacticians or politicians, not sure which one. Pilots would call it covering their "six."

The air space over the Bay of Pigs was now controlled by Castro's air power. Castro's jet powered T-33s, in concert with equally nimble piston-driven British-made Sea Fury, shot down five of the less-agile B-26s without incurring any losses of their own. Without air cover, the invading brigade did not have a chance for success. After three days of fighting, with depleted supplies, and being surrounded, they had no other alternative but to surrender. The failure to destroy Castro's air force on the ground left the flotilla vulnerable to enemy air attacks. This criminal decision led to the flotilla's supply ship carrying reinforcements, ammunition, food, and medical provisions defenseless and blown out of the water by Castro's air force. When the news of Castro's victory arrived in Havana, Marco knew that his dream of staying home with his parents was dead and buried. Might as well erect a tombstone on the beaches of the Bay of Pigs and move on.

Throughout the raid, Marco's dad was in Havana, working the night shift in his uncle Armando's *quiosco*, a small stand-up café with no tables, which was popular in Cuba. Customers purchased strong Cuban coffee, cigarettes, and *bocadillos*, a small sandwich among other items.

Cubans, if anything, are grand raconteurs. The story can always be embellished to entertain the listener. The word was out that the neighborhood where his family lived had been completely wiped out during the air raid. His dad was devastated. He took whatever transportation was available home.

After the attack, people slowly and carefully started walking out of their homes. The first thing Marco saw was the black plume of smoke that covered the horizon. Neighbors got together and thanked God that everyone was safe. About this time, Marco saw his dad at the beginning of the street where a bus had dropped him off. He just stood there looking in the direction of his home and ran toward his family, hugging his wife and son like they had been resurrected from the dead.

CHAPTER 9

It was settled, no looking back. Marco was going to New York following the invasion's crushing defeat. The complex and expensive travel paperwork took months to complete. One had to be extremely careful, for the government could suspend one's travel plans for any perceived or fabricated infraction. A passport, pictures, vaccinations, Catholic Relief Service permission letter, and his aunt's reclamation from the United States—all this administrative nightmare must be completed before the Cuban government would even review his travel plan.

Of paramount importance was the inventory of household goods. Once your intention to leave the country became known, all your property would revert to the government. Government officials came to your home, armed with a notebook and pen cataloging every item in the house. Furniture, curtains, television, radio, refrigerator, pots and pans, clothes, in short—everything was compiled and filed away.

Marco's travel to the United States was approved on 18 September 1961. KLM Royal Dutch Airlines, notified the José Martí airport in Rancho Boyeros, Havana, that they had been notified via their office in Miami that Marco was authorized to travel to Miami without the required visa stamp on his passport—the Peter Pan Project working. A few days later, on 9 October 1961, his aunt provided the necessary funds to the Banco Nacional de Cuba for his trip.

Finally, 15 December 1961 arrived, the travel day to Miami. His mother had him dressed in a new suit, tie, and shoes. The loudspeaker announced that the KLM flight to the US was boarding. He felt that his life was being cut at its roots. He felt like a boy without country, without family, without friends. In the passageway leading to the aircraft, there was a large window separating passengers from non-travelers. Marco placed his hand on the window, and so did his Mom. They held their hands on the window for a few seconds before the tide of passengers boarding the plane took him along like human flotsam.

CHAPTER 10

Following the precedence set by millions of immigrant families, Marco's aunt and uncle worked hard and saved their money. One day, with enough savings set aside, the four of them moved to the top floor of a large private home on Irving Avenue. This was a long way from South Main Street. Peace and quiet replaced the constant hustle and bustle of downtown Port Chester. The South Main Street apartment was rented by a newly arrived family member. The apartment was only ninety dollars per month, the affordable starter dwelling place for newcomers to the United States.

The new apartment had two bedrooms, one bath, a living room, a kitchen, and a small room that fit a single bed, which now became Marco's tiny "bedroom." Small steps in the American way, but things were looking up when once dismal. Marco was learning life lessons that he would retain as he got older.

Marco was studying and playing sports with his new friends. With Jimmy, Godfrey, Bernie, Gary, and Joey, the guys got together every day to talk, play, or hang out. Marco wanted to be assimilated, be one of the guys, but in reality, more than anything, he wanted to roam centerfield like his idols Mays and Mantle.

He also noticed that most of his friends identified themselves as either "Irish" or "Italian." This did not make sense to him. Where they not born in the United States?

It took time, but Marco was understanding the American way—the great melting pot of races, creeds, and cultures. At home, Marco spoke Spanish, ate Cuban food, and lived the Cuban culture. Outside, he followed the norms, culture, and language of America. That was exactly what his "Irish" and "Italian" friends were also practicing.

Marco understood that one reason America was powerful and united was because English was spoken from Maine to California. One language, one culture. Unlike in Europe, where if you traveled for say two hundred miles in any direction, different languages and cultures abounded. What a wonderful land to live in and be a member. In the United States, you could express yourself without fear of being execrated as was the case in communist Cuba.

CHAPTER 11

At last, after many months of waiting in Limbo, Marco's parents were given permission to apply for travel to the US. Again, the mountain of paperwork lay ahead. One more time, government official arrived at Marco's house with inventory in hand. The same inventory used for Marco's travel. One curtain was found missing, which they claimed "stolen." The inspection was stopped on its tracks and would not resume until the missing curtain reappeared. His mom knew exactly where the curtain resided: with her mother. The curtain was returned to its proper place, and the authorities notified.

His mom thought, *In this populist regime, everything belongs to the people. If everyone owned everything, then, of course, no one owned anything. So how could it be theft if no one owned it?* It was, in reality, a conundrum that government officials manipulated for their own benefit.

Marco's parents arrived in the US in late summer 1962. The family moved into the same old 15 South Main Street address he shared with his aunt and uncle when he first arrived in December 1961.

Living with his parents was comforting. He was king of the household again. His parents found work at factories, making the minimum wage of the era, a dollar and fifteen cents an hour, and they were grateful that employment provided independence to choose their path.

His dad was a skillful barber, his mom an equally terrific seamstress. While his dad cut hair on the side, his mom made dresses on the other. Little by little, they saved their hard-earned money and made their lives better.

His parents were in their midforties when they arrived in the US. They did not speak English or knew the culture and, at best, had a sixth-grade education. But they had pride, a superlative work ethic, and a common-sense PhD.

The next few months also had some fun adventures. One night, a fire broke out in one of the apartments. A man fell asleep with a lit cigarette. The blanket caught fire, and so did his bedroom. Smoke started billowing out of his place, and in short order, the smoke consumed the tenement building. Thankfully, the fire department had a rescue unit across the street and were fighting the blaze lickity split. The firemen went about door-to-door, sounding the alarm that the building was on fire.

Unfamiliar with the English language, Marco's parents thought that robbers were trying to steal their meager belongings. Marco had to explain, as smoke creeped under the door, that the people at the door were firemen and that the building was on fire. At last, he got his message across. They quickly threw some clothes on and went outside where the sidewalk was covered with snow and ice. The firemen swiftly got the blaze under control, and all residents went back into their apartments, but not without a stern warning—no smoking in bed!

One fine day, a handsome young man appeared in their tenement building, offering free English lessons. At the time, there were two other Cuban families living in the building. The male spouses had also served in Batista's military. Next thing you know, a classroom was set up. A small blackboard, chalk, and eraser appeared from nowhere. The handsome young man brought basic English books. Soon, a full complement of students, including the wives, joined the party. Marco's mom brewed Cuban coffee, and she always had snacks to munch on too. His mom also thought that the handsome young man was too skinny, so she made it her goal to fatten him up. Well, this went on for several weeks until, for days, the handsome young man failed to show up.

Everyone was puzzled by his disappearance. Hadn't they all been attending his lectures, brewing coffee, providing snacks, and even feeding him black beans and rice to fatten him up? Finally, it dawned on them that the handsome young man was probably an FBI agent. His mission was to test their loyalty to the United States. Once he was satisfied that there were no Castro sympathizers in the group, that they all detested communism and loved democracy, his mission was complete. They all had a good laugh and admired the United States even more.

The first floor of the tenement was the site of the Blue Rail, a swinging tavern. The Blue Rail came to life at night. Upstairs, in his apartment, Marco heard the wonderful music coming from the never-resting jukebox. He became familiar with all the sounds of the era: Elvis's "Can't Help Falling in Love," The Shirelles's "Baby It's You," Isley Brothers' "Twist and Shout," Jay and the Americans' "She Cried," Ray Charles's "I Can't Stop Loving You," and so many other tunes.

The tavern had a really cool neon sign on its window of a martini glass topped off with an olive. Marco was still quite short, so he could not reach high enough to see inside. He got on his tippy-toes attempting to take a peek, but it was to no avail. He could only imagine what the establishment looked like on the inside. Then it happened: the Blue Rail was raided by the vice squad. No more music, no more wondering what was happening inside. It turned out the tavern, in addition to serving food and liquor, was also serving a dish that never gets old. The Blue Rail was also a brothel!

On December 24, Cubans celebrate the *Noche Buena* (literally translated the "Good Night"). It is a food-and-drink feast shared with family and friends. It is also a time to reflect and a time to look ahead. At the appropriate time, Marco's father raised his glass and invited his mom and him to raise theirs as well. The glasses were filled with wine, even Marco's, although his glass only had a little wine. His dad toasted to the following, "El año que viene, el La Habana," which meant "next year in Havana."

CHAPTER 12

The family moved to Poningo Street sometime in 1963, a semi-residential neighborhood. A couple of small factories nearby and private business also doted the landscape. The apartment had a single bedroom, bath, kitchen, living room, and a small flower garden.

His school was a lot closer. A couple of blocks up Irving Avenue past the junior high on the right, then left by the library, cross Westchester Avenue, and he was at the school. OLM had a large fenced in parking lot that doubled as a recreational area. Softball, football, and basketball were all played in that lot.

One afternoon, Marco was shooting baskets by himself. Walking toward him was a boy and a lady. The boy Roberto turned out to be Cuban. He came from the eastern part of the island where they spoke Spanish with a different accent from Havana. They immediately hit it off and became friends. A few weeks passed, and he met another Cuban boy, named Mario. The three of them became good buddies.

One afternoon, Marco ran home; he was looking forward to talking to his parents and telling them the wonderful news. Tired from work, his mom and dad were ready to relax a bit before starting the evening meal. Marco said to them:

"The government gives free money. You don't have to work. It is called welfare."

His mom and dad looked at each other and gently asked him to sit and to listen.

"Son, not working is a disgrace when you are healthy. We did not come to the US to to accept charity from the government. We are grateful for the opportunity this country has given us to work and make our own way. When the government gives you something that you have not earned, you place little value on it and expect even more. When you work, you earn a salary, and you can buy anything. You value your purchases because you earned them and not because it was given to you. If it is given, redistributed in the government's case, it is ephemeral. Like smoke, it disappears in a short time, and now you depend on the government to provide for your subsistence. Never forget, there is nothing free in this world. Someone somehow is paying for 'free' stuff."

Marco rode his bike all over Port Chester, learning the village's nook and crannies. This was an era when kids went about exploring by themselves without fear of someone harming them. For working moms, it was reassuring that their kids would be safe in a club like Catholic Youth Organization (CYO). Here, kids watched TV, bounced on a trampoline, listened to music, played pool, basketball, dodgeball; they were kept busy and out of trouble. Also, they socialized with other kids and CYO adult supervisors.

He also played Little League Baseball for the Catholic Youth Program (CYP) Greens. A team that somehow managed to lose every game even though it had some pretty good ballplayers.

Lyons Park was one of several ballfields where he played Little League games. The park had two fields. On this occasion, a pickup game against rival kids was quickly assembled between the two groups. In those days, this form of planning was routine, no need for parents to take the kids to the park by car and supervise the date. Marco rode his bike with the bat across the handle bars and the glove securely hanging from the same.

One of the kids, a puerile whippersnapper, brought hard chewing tobacco to the game. He said that this was what real ballplayers chewed. Marco took the plug and gnawed at it, producing a strong tobacco scent, which he did not really enjoy, but, hey, this is what real ballplayers do.

They were like the professional players, they thought, and Marco took ground balls at shortstop, the position he was playing that day, all the while the chaw of tobacco bulging his cheek like he had seen ballplayers on TV. He took some balls to his right, some to his left, and practiced turning over a double play. It was almost the end of practice when he took a bad hop to the chest, swallowed the disgusting chew, turned into a kaleidoscope of colors, and deposited the contents in his stomach on the infield dirt. Sometimes it is not the physical pain that hurts the most, but the psychological embarrassment that takes the biggest toll on the already shaky self-confidence of an adolescent boy. He heard his buddy's laughter, some of them holding their bellies as they rolled on the grass in complete joy and away from the offending discharge. They all moved to the other clean field and played their game. Marco recovered and took the field.

Things were not always rosy at home. Marco stood between his parents as they argued for the hundredth time. His dad told his mom to pack his things because he was leaving. His mom's reply was, "Pack it yourself." He told them it would be best if they separated, that he would spend time with both of them because he loved them both.

Marco's father was a handsome man. When Marco's family still lived in Cuba, his father was unfaithful to his mother on many occasions. Years later when Marco was a grown man his father told him "it takes more guts to say no to a woman's wink than to go along and say yes." But that is, perhaps, a story for another time.

Marco recalled how his mom took him by the hand and went looking for an apartment for the two of them. It took courage for a woman to walk away from her husband and forge a new life in what was a macho and Catholic Cuba in the 1950s, but she had plenty of courage and had enough of his infidelities. Now on his knees begging for forgiveness and promising to never stray again, she reluctantly took him back a few days later.

Marco's mom was five foot four, medium built, and with a beautiful face. The most prominent feature were her large hazel eyes, with determination and self-reliance written all over them.

His mother learned what suffering was all about at a tender age of seven. Her father was a successful business man. He owned a bus line, cattle, farmland, and a number of smaller businesses. In 1927, at the age of forty, he died following an appendectomy. The surgery was a success, but as it was often the case at that time, post-surgery infection was the real killer, and that is what happened to his grandfather. Overcome with grief, Marco's grandmother fell into a deep depression, unable to cope with the reality that her husband was gone and with the dire family situation. Unscrupulous family members stole her dad's wealth, leaving nothing for her mom and siblings.

So with the passage of time, living through a communist revolution and now living in the US, they were back in the same old predicament. Somehow, they managed a fragile truce and continued married life for fifty-nine years. His dad passed away in 1999.

CHAPTER 13

Marco walked home in a little bit of trepidation. He carried a note from the school principal. The note was just a piece of paper in an envelope, yet it felt like a hundred pounds in his pocket. Assuredly, the note did not bring good news. He gave the letter to his mom and translated it into Spanish. Her reaction was completely unexpected. The first thing she said was, "How could you do this to God's wife!" He was not sure God was married, for he had not learned that in catechism or from la Señora Gretel.

The note said that Marco was a smart boy, but he was not working hard enough in his schoolwork—that he was more interested in playing sports and socializing. His mother told him to write down a response. He did, writing down exactly what his mom had dictated.

The next morning, he handed the note to the principal. She looked down at him. She was much taller. She spoke and sounded as if her voice came from heaven. She bonked him on the head and said that he had good parents.

Time for redemption, soul cleansing after the last few days of scholastic torture now that the teachers had carte blanche to do with him as required to make him study. The solution came in the form of preparation for Confirmation, one of the seven sacraments of the Catholic Church. The other sacraments are Baptism, Eucharist, Reconciliation, Anointing of the Sick, Marriage, and Holy Orders. Marco learned the fundamentals of Catholicism from la Señora Gretel.

She was a housewife with five children. She was a neighbor. She spoke softly, intelligently, and was respected by all. She cared for the spiritual education of all, and she prepared all kids in the Marianao

neighborhood for their First Communion. She had a special connection with God, and she had laid out a solid foundation that prepared
Marco well for his upcoming Confirmation.

CHAPTER 14

October is a beautiful month, when fall lights up the landscape with a kaleidoscope of colors as leaves slowly withered and die, but not before providing the canvass for a masterful painting. It is also a reminder that winter lies ahead with its shivering cold, snow, and ice. In 1962, October trumpeted more than a change of seasons. War was in the horizon, and Cuba, under communist leadership, was the main instigator, the protagonist of nightmarish tragicomedy leading the world toward Armageddon.

The US and USSR were nose-to-nose in one of the defining moments in history. The Soviets' stealthily deployed nuclear missiles into Cuba, but their gamble was discovered by US intelligence services. The two superpowers were trapped like a grain between two millstones. Somehow, both powers had to save face before the world's critics.

Like millions of families, Marco's parents watched the apocalyptic melodrama unfold on TV, aggravating their taut nerves like a dripping faucet. For sure, this confrontation was the straw that broke the camel's back. In the last eighteen months, Cuba's anti-American actions and rhetoric had been a thorny issue to US political and diplomatic arena. First, the failure of the Bay of Pigs invasion, and now this face-off between the two most powerful nuclear powers on the globe. There was no way the US would allow tiny Cuba to throw dirt on the colossal US face. Kennedy would not let Castro keep nuclear missiles only ninety miles from American shores. The Castro days were numbered; his parents were convinced that their Christmas toast, "El Año que viene en La Habana," would come true.

Not so fast, Cuba became a pounding migraine headache for the US for many years to come. His parents, though disappointed that Castro was still in power, were happy the crisis was resolved and that the USSR took back the nuclear missiles they had planted on Cuban soil. They understood that 1963 would not be the year of repatriation.

Repatriation would not happen 1964 either. While sitting in class in late November 1963, the school principal spoke over the loudspeaker, interrupting a civics lesson. She asked for everyone's prayers. President Kennedy had been shot in Dallas, Texas. A few minutes later, she was back on the loudspeaker to announce that President Kennedy died. She said a prayer for his soul and for his family. School was dismissed early. It was a somber walk home for Marco.

CHAPTER 15

Violence does not respect borders. The daily skirmishes between the counterrevolutionaries and the police became more and more bloody. Drive-by shootings, pipe bombs, Molotov cocktails, and petards—all these were the weapons of the counterrevolutionaries. They moved from safe house to safe house. Sometimes in the trunks of cars, they wore disguises and planned their next move to disrupt Castro's power base.

Marco's parents decided to have him spend time with his aunt and uncle in Santa Clara province until the violence cooled down in Havana. His mom packed a travel bag and took him to his grandmother's apartment in Lawton where his aunt Emelina was visiting her mother. Early the next day, him and his aunt walked to the bus terminal. Aunt Emelina saw a young man walking by and asked him to help carry the luggage. He helped carry the luggage, and she gave him a few pesos, Cuban currency, for his efforts.

The bus ride was several hours long. Cuban infrastructure was still adequate in 1960. Marco had never been to that part of the island, and he marveled at the beauty of the scenery before him. Emerald-green rolling hills, banana trees, and royal palms that grow forty to sixty feet tall. He saw multicolored birds, big and small, that he had never seen before. At a rest stop, he saw a huge iguana. A crocodile, with its mouth opened taking in the sun's warmth, relaxed in its pen. To Marco, it seemed the croc was as large as the bus that was carrying them to their destination.

Change often comes from within, not from without. His *tio* (uncle) Alegret was well indoctrinated in Marxist philosophy—a true believer. *Tio* Alegret had been a soldier in Batista's army. Smart, charismatic, and handsome, he stealthily and skillfully risked his life to create disloyalty in Batista's armed forces. He was very good at his craft.

When Castro came to power, he was duly rewarded. He was given a beautiful home and promoted to party boss in a Santa Clara district. The house had a warm, old Spanish feel to it. In the center of the house, there was a large garden with exquisite Spanish tile around its border where Marco and his cousin Viviane played. All rooms seemed to flow into the garden.

Marco liked his uncle, a lot. Who would not like a smart and fun guy? Sometimes his uncle would take him for a walk in his district. *Camarada* this and *camarada* that, said the sycophants hurrying to kiss his uncle's ring. *Camarada* means comrade in Spanish. One night, as they walked on a beautiful moonlit night, an especially bootlicking *camarada* with a sallow face, with bushy eyebrows, and red watery eyes said to his uncle:

"I see your training your young nephew into the ways of Marxism."

Tio Alegret responded, with a sly smile:

"No, not this one. There is no convincing him. This one is completely bourgeois." A few weeks later, Marco was back with his parents as the violence in Havana had been abated by harsh police tactics.

CHAPTER 16

On a cold December night, the family gathered in the warmth of his aunt's apartment. There was food, drink, and lots of music as aunts and uncles and cousins enjoyed a family get-together.

This was a time when most adults smoked cigarettes and cigars. His uncle Pedro was a big cigar smoker. A fun night of family chaos punctuated by dancing, eating, drinking, and everyone talking at the same time. Uncle Pedro put down his freshly lit cigar on an ashtray. Marco looked at the small roll of tobacco leaf with inquisitive eyes. His dad noticed his son and said, "Pick it up, and put it to your mouth." So he did. Then his dad said, "Now inhale it." So he did.

After a prolonged coughing fit, his dad said, "Inhale it again. It takes a little getting used to." So he did. Marco turned green, felt nauseous, and ran to the bathroom, where he spent the next few minutes holding on to the commode as if it were his best friend; he felt as if his internal organs were exiting their assigned location with each violent heave. Marco would never go near a cigar again—lesson learned. The score now stood: two for tobacco, zero for Marco.

Opportunity is fleeting, and so is help from human guardian angel. Marco was fortunate to have such an angel on his corner that provided him with opportunity. He did not miss the chance.

Just as predicted by the school principal, Marco barely got by in his studies. The high school years were just around the bend. Like so many of his buddies, he applied to Archbishop Stepinac High School in White Plains, New York. He did not make the grade. He only made the school's waiting list. Instead, he would have to go to Port Chester Junior High.

Sister Regina saw Marco's sadness. She said, "Would you like to go to Stepinac?" His reply was yes. "You have to promise me that you will try harder with your studies." He said that he would try harder. Sister Regina must have been highly respected, for Marco was accepted to Stepinac. He would attend high school with his buddies Jimmy, Godfrey, and Bernie. He was still one of the boys. He was happy and extremely grateful to Sister Regina.

It was September 1965. Marco was now a freshman at the Archbishop Stepinac High School. The school had a practice of measuring and weighing students at the start of the new school year. Marco came in at 5 foot 2 inches and 110 pounds. His mother told him a while back that he would be 6 foot tall, just like his dad. He had his doubts.

The school year passed uneventful. He walked to the bus stop, which was behind the public library just a few blocks from his home. It was an all-boys catholic high school where students were required to wear a jacket and tie. The grooming rules were strictly adhered to no long sideburns, and no facial or long hair.

When he was weighed and measured at the beginning of his sophomore year, he tipped the scales at 120 pounds and had grown to 5 foot 9 inches. Throughout the school year and into the summer, Marco had aches and pains on his knees and legs. Was he experiencing "growing pains?" Who knew? Maybe he would grow to be 6 foot tall after all.

Sophomore year was pretty uneventful too. He played center field on the J. V. Baseball Team. He had an okay year, nothing great. His grades were not good, but they were not bad either. He was only getting by. Again, he was not pursuing his studies as he should. The year's biggest thrill was when he turned sixteen, now eligible to take the driver's written test, which he promptly passed.

CHAPTER 17

Sitting on the driver's seat of the '57 DeSoto, a recent purchase by his parents, he turned the key and started the colossus. He felt the power of two hundred horses under his feet. He adjusted to seat and mirrors and held the steering wheel, feeling like Mario Andretti.

He only had a driver's permit, but his mom and dad let him take the wheel on every opportunity. Before long, he felt expert enough to take the driver's test, which he passed with flying colors. He could only drive during daylight hours since he did not take the driver's education course. One must at least eighteen to drive at night. On occasion, he came home after sunset, but not too often.

About this time, he discovered girls. As he moved into adolescence, he no longer responded to the booming hormones by joining the Boy Scouts; instead, he looked forward to necking and petting.

Lucy was a great ice-skater with pretty legs. Kimmie had big, beautiful blue eyes, a tiny nose, and freckles. Sarah was pretty, smart, and had a terrific sense of humor. He knew these girls liked him, but in addition to being shy around girls, his confidence was lacking. His conscience spun him like a kite dancing in a hurricane. His mom said, "Respect girls at all times." His dad said, "Enjoy the company of girls, for there is nothing better."

One warm Sunday afternoon, Laurie, with her long auburn hair and big brown eyes, kissed him like he had never been kissed before. A bolt of lightning struck from the top of his head and all the way down to his toes. She put him in a trance. Maybe his father was right after all. He took her to the junior prom, where he saw Lucy dancing with someone else. He felt a little bit jealous. *Maybe I am growing up*, he thought.

That summer, he got a job as a stock boy at E. J. Korvettes. He had left behind a job cleaning offices. With a little pocket money, he could put gas in the car and occasionally go out on a date to the movies or just ride around until it was time to put more gas in the car. Gasoline cost about twenty-five cents per gallon in the late 1960s.

His dad's brother brought his family to live in Port Chester. His uncle Alberto bought the DeSoto, and his parents then upgraded to a used 1962 Chevy Impala. It was a baby-blue two-door car, and it made a sweet sound with its Glasspack Muffler. He felt like, "Now we are talking. Here I come, baby." It is amazing the pull a car has over a teenage boy.

Every legal immigrant dreamed of working at Arnold's Bakery. The starting hourly salary was $2.00. With his mom now working at a local factory earning $1.75 per hour, the family finances kept improving. It was time for a move.

Grove Street was dotted with residential homes, no small businesses, and it was peaceful. The home had two bedrooms, one bath, a kitchen, living room, small enclosed patio provided for much more comfortable living space, plus a garage. It also meant that finally, at the age fourteen, Marco had his own room. He could not believe his good fortune.

His parents walked to work. However, Arnold's was building a much larger and modern plant in Greenwich, Connecticut, that would be ready for business in a few months. It was about a ten-minute car ride from their home.

His dad was making positive strides at work. Although he lacked a high school education—in fact, he lacked a grammar school education...—he was but a born leader. The man exuded leadership. He was promoted to foreman because he inspired people to work with gusto. He got things done.

In the meantime, his mom was buying household goods to take back to Cuba when Castro fell from power. His parents had a theory that Cuban dictators lasted in place between five to seven years. Soon Castro would be gone, and the family repatriated in Havana.

With his dad working in Greenwich, Arnold's factory had moved from Port Chester, and with his family owning only one car, Marco routinely picked up his dad at work. It was a hot late afternoon, and the Chevy did not have air-conditioning. Marco was sweating bullets on this hot, humid afternoon while he waited for his father to walk out.

Four men strode out of the factory, and they were laughing. His dad was one of them. They continued the conversation a dozen feet from the car. They all spoke simultaneously with lots of hand gestures. Marco did not understand a word they were saying, but they sure were having a heck of a good time.

His dad sat down in the car, still enjoying the fun time with his buddies. Marco asked, "What language were you guys speaking?"

"English, of course."

"No, no, that was not English, but whatever it was, you guys understood each other."

CHAPTER 18

With the new year 1967, Marco was sensing a new and strong calling from within. He loved and respected his Spanish heritage and customs. His ancestor went to Cuba from Leon, a city in northern Spain, and Barcelona, the great port city in northeastern Spain. However, now he was feeling more like a New Yorker than a *Habanero*, a person from Havana. He sensed a connection with the New York Mets and Jets that was akin to marriage. He liked the snow and cold and the fast pace of New York.

His aunt and uncle moved to a bigger house in Rye, New York, because they needed the extra room. Marco's grandmother had immigrated to the United States and was now living in Rye with his aunt and uncle. All of Marco's aunts and uncles were now safely out Cuba. The exception being his aunt Emelina and uncle Alegret. They were part of the Cuban nomenklatura, enjoying the benefits bestowed on that elite socialist class.

His aunt had a big birthday party that also doubled to cheer his grandmother's arrival. Friends and family gather at the Rye house for the celebration. There was an abundance of food, drink, and lots of Cuban music. The party ensued the entire night with people dancing and, of course, in good Cuban style, everyone speaking at the same time.

The joyous scene also captured Marco's enthusiasm. He had little wine, then a little rum, then a little more wine and rum. His parents watched and allowed him to self-destruct. Marco was dancing—he loved to dance—when suddenly he just did not feel right. He went upstairs to Randy's room. The laughter and the music wafted upstairs where he was hoping to rest. He laid down on the bed. The room started spinning. He put one leg on the carpet, hoping to stop the room from spinning, but that did not work. He felt sick to his stomach. No time to run to the bathroom. Out came the contents in his stomach. He tried to clean up the mess using his cousin's tee shirts, which he had taken from the dresser drawer. His parents walked up to the room and saw the wreck that was their son.

As his parents walked him out of the house and to the car, Marco heard people laughing at his inebriated state. He had no alternative but take the jeering and move on. Right then and there, he promised himself he would never again let himself fall into that situation ever, ever again. The next morning, his parents served him breakfast in bed. Along with luscious scrambled eggs and toast, there was a brand-new bottle of Bacardi rum. He lost his appetite.

Italian fairs season was in full steam. Port Chester, Rye, Harrison, and other villages honored their saints with a great feast. The fair celebrated a particular saint associated to that town or village. Carnival rides, music, skill competition, and food and lots and lots of savory Italian cuisine were available. Meatball, sausages, baked goods—it was a banquet with no equal. It was also an opportunity to check out girls other than the ones in Port Chester. It was truly an all-American feast hosted by Italian Americans.

Rye was home to Playland, a little version of Disneyland. One could spend the entire day on fun rides, eating, drinking, playing miniature golf, and all in a beautiful setting. Playland was located on a strip of land next to Long Island Sound. One could easily look across the sound and see the island. The complex had its own beach and swimming pool. It was a paradise for young, old, and everyone in between.

Marco and the guys spent a lot of time on the beach. So good to be young. You work, go to the beach, stay out late, and you do it all again the next day. One of the guys was an aspiring bodybuilder and handsome to boot. Once they parked the cars, this nutty guy would drop on the deck and start doing push-ups, wanting to be pumped up in front of the girls, while the rest of the guys just sucked in their stomachs. The amazing result was that it actually worked most of the time. The girls wanted to touch his bulging biceps. All the guys shook their heads in disbelief of what took place in plain view.

One late summer afternoon, just before his senior year started, he met Julie. She had the prettiest eyes he had ever seen; she was smart and affectionate. Soon they were dating, then "going steady." They were inseparable.

As 1968 ended, things were looking up. Along with a great relationship with Julie, his parents bought him a brand-new Firebird 350 midnight blue-and-white interior. School was going just fine. Julie's dad had season tickets to Jets games. He attended the Jets-Raiders championship game at Shea Stadium. The Jets won a thrilling game and went to the Super Bowl to face the mighty Baltimore Colts.

On a somber note, his parents finally accepted they were not going back to Cuba. Castro was firmly entrenched in Cuba; he was not going anywhere.

"El año que viene en La Habana" now sounded hollow and uninspiring. There was time that he looked forward to returning to Cuba, but just like seasons change, he was changing too. He was born in Cuba, but now in his mind and heart, he was an American!

CHAPTER 19

The new year 1969 was special. The Jets won the Super Bowl, the Mets won the World Series, he graduated high school, and in the fall, he was going to be a freshman at Marist College.

The Jets and Mets victories had a huge impression on the way he approached challenges. The Jets were huge underdogs against the awesome Baltimore Colts, likewise, the Mets underdogs against the better Baltimore Orioles. Yet both New York teams defeated the superior Baltimore teams. As an immigrant that had to learn English and a new culture, he felt like an underdog, but just like his teams, he too could succeed in this great land of opportunity.

His senior year was much more than an academic experience. It was maturation as an individual. He learned from his girlfriend's mom the gift of sharing. Her mom was one of the people he most admired. She was patient, smart, forgiving, and an outstanding cook and baker.

Her home was always redolent of savory Italian cuisine. Sausage and meatball, lasagna, penne, and so many other dishes made your mouth water. Marco now eating more than ever before yet still incapable of putting on pounds on his six-foot frame. He started thinking that the stork had made a wrong turn when she delivered him on an island. Instead, she should have delivered him on a boot, Italy.

He also turned eighteen during the school year and dutifully registered with the local draft board. Legal aliens were allowed to serve in the military, and Marco was willing to serve. As a legal alien, about the only privilege he did not have was the right to vote. That right and privilege was reserved, and rightly so, he thought, for American citizens only.

As the school year was coming to an end, Marco and his buddies prepared for the senior prom. They rented tuxedos, bought corsages, and hired a limousine chauffer to take them to the Glenn Island Casino, the prom's venue.

The limo could easily hold three couples, but Jimmy got sick and cancelled. Marco and Julie and Jeff and Cindy now had the entire limo to themselves. After much dancing and socializing, they went to the Copacabana, or just plain Copa, in New York City. They tipped the maître d' and went inside and were lucky to get a table close to the stage where Smokey Robinson and the Miracles were performing. Smokey and the Miracles sang and danced to their all hits. It was impossible to sit still. Marco danced along with the Miracles and even got some applause from the patronage.

The limo driver took them to Julie's house where their cars waited for them. Performing his morning ablutions, a change of clothes, a beach towel, and some Coppertone, Marco picked up Julie, and off they went to Jones Beach in Long Island.. Crossed the Whitestone Bridge and eventually unto the Long Island Expressway (LIE), sometimes called the largest parking lot in the world because of its nightmarish traffic jams. At last, Jones Beach, sand and salt-water to spare. After frolicking in the water, everyone was exhausted from the previous fun night and long drive to the beach. Before long, everyone was asleep.

The way home felt like being in a hot, humid, sweaty, sandy pipe while traveling at a snail's pace in a car without air-conditioning (AC). They were back on the LIE. In this traffic, you could not take advantage of four-seventy AC. Roll all four windows down, and do seventy!

PART II

CHAPTER 1

That summer, Marco moved up in the job world. He started working for Learned and Patterson Tree Service, at the princely sum of $2.50 an hour. With his earnings, he bought new clothes for the coming year at Marist and kept the Firebird gassed up. He still had enough money to routinely take Julie out to dinner and a movie.

Summer quickly turned into fall. It was time to head to Poughkeepsie and Marist. He arrived at the college in late August 1969, and it was beastly hot. His dorm room was 215 Sheehan Hall, and his roommate was great guy from New Jersey, named Marty. Marty was a psychology major, Marco a Spanish major. Marty was also a terrific football player. He had been scouted by big time football schools like Nebraska and Oklahoma, but a bad concussion during practice in his senior year in high school kept him from reaching his full potential, and the football recruiters vanished.

Marco regressed in his studies, again doing the minimum to get by. He made some terrific new friends, however: Carmine, Boder, Michael, Lenny, and above all Tommy. Carmine was a bit of a Bolshevik, but he liked him. Boder was a capitalist that roomed with Carmine, but they got along like two peas in a pod. It was fun to listen to them debate the two different political philosophies.

Michael, Lenny, and Tommy were Spanish majors. Tommy was also a terrific athlete, handsome, and just a great guy. He loved the song "The Worst That Could Happen" by the Brooklyn Bridge and could be heard singing or humming it quite often.

On Friday afternoons, Julie's mom would pick up Marco at Marist. On Sunday night, Marco's mom would take him back to the school. This ritual continued throughout his freshman year, for first year students were not allowed to have a car on campus, and Marco wanted to spend time with Julie.

One night, all the guys gathered in the basement of Sheehan Hall to watch the military draft drawing. The small black-and-white TV screen flickered like it had a bad case of indigestion. Marco's number was in the high two hundreds, so he was pretty safe from being drafted. However, a couple of his friends drew low numbers and would certainly be gone at the end of the semester, reporting to their local induction center a short time later.

Nobody talked about running to Canada with their tails between their legs to avoid serving. Everyone understood that if they ran to Canada, some other man would have to take their place.

Since 1962, Marco and his family registered their legal alien status at the post office. His parents now looked forward to becoming American citizens since repatriation to Cuba was out of the question. Castro was not going anywhere. It required time for the citizenship paperwork to work its way through the immigration process.

On 21 April 1970, Marco received a United States Department of Justice card acknowledging his filing for petition for naturalization. At the appointed time, he was to report at the Supreme Court, White Plains, New York.

A few months later, 31 July 1970, he received a letter from his congressman Ogden Reid congratulating him as a new citizen of the United States. He reminded Marco that one of the most sacred privileges of an American citizen was the right to vote. Marco clearly understood that voting was a right reserved for citizens, and only citizens.

CHAPTER 2

Second semester freshman year was much more successful than the first. He finished the year with a 2.9 cumulative grade in a 4.0 scale.

Marco tried out for the football team during spring practice. Marty had a stellar football year in the fall, playing for Marist, and bigtime football scouts were back trying to recruit him for their programs. Tommy was a terrific wide receiver, fast and with great hands. Marco had always had a good, strong throwing arm and was elusive. He was also 140 pounds. It was not long before he was hurt, and so came the end of his football career.

Late April and early May 1970 was a time of controversy and tension in the country. The Vietnam War continued to escalate, and dissent and protest against the war took main stage in many colleges campuses throughout the land. Then all hell broke loose in Kent State University.

The Kent State shootings occurred during a mass protest against the bombing of Cambodia by the US Military. On 4 May 1970, four students were shot and killed by Ohio National Guardsman sent to the university to quell the demonstration. The result was massive protests throughout college campuses that included Marist. The school's administrators appeared paralyzed in a state of panic.

While Marist's administrators hesitated on what to do next, Marco and seven other guys decided to take a canoe trip. They rented two canoes and paddled up the Hudson River. Crossed the river from the east side to the west side. Alighted on the west bank to rest. The Hudson is pretty wide in that area and still a bit cold in early May.

They continued paddling north in the direction of Hyde Park, this time racing. Marco's boat lagged well behind the stronger and better rowers. As they were crossing back toward the eastern bank of the river, the wind picked up, making the crossing treacherous.

Marco's boat made it safely across the wide breadth of the river. All the guys wet and cold. Marco followed the railroad tracks going north toward Hyde Park to meet up with his buddies. He saw what looked like a person in the water, picked up the pace, and then started running. He heard a cry for help, and then he saw one of his friends a few feet from the shore and another scrambling unto dry land. Their canoe had taken on water and somehow capsized.

Marco ran up and down the riverbank looking for his friends. One by one, they all made it ashore, except for Tommy. The search for Tommy intensified everyone looking for and yelling his name. The search continued with professional help from local firemen and emergency trained personnel. The search was canceled many hours later. It was to no avail. Tommy was gone.

Marty and Marco now back in their dorm were experiencing remorse. Why Tommy, why not one of them? Tommy was by far the best athlete, the kindest, the most liked and admired. His optimistic outlook, ready laughter, intelligence, and willingness to help others would be sorely missed.

Weeks passed, and Tommy's body finally surfaced near West Point. He was buried in Long Island. At last, he could rest in peace. For Marco, it was "The Worst That Could Happen."

CHAPTER 3

That summer was not memorable. He and Julie continued to "go steady." He played in a softball league and back at work at Learned and Patterson. He drove an old truck that pulled a wood chipper. All the guys he worked with were professionals. They knew how to take proper care of trees, lawns, and gardens. Marco fed the wood chipper for eight hours. The chipping duties must have been some sort of work trial because once he passed their test, they started teaching him the finer methods of the business.

Toward the end of the summer, Marco had surgery on his left knee to remove a cyst and meniscus. He spent several days in the hospital. A cast from his toes all the way to upper thigh now dressed his leg. He had lost weight while convalescing. In his pale six-foot frame, he resembled a scarecrow.

Now his sophomore year was underway, and he was back in Sheehan Hall with his roommate Marty. He got around with the aid of crutches. The cast on his leg made mobility difficult. He developed a rash under his arm from the crutches' constant rubbing and was an utterly miserable young man.

Walking to class, the cafeteria, or just going from his room to the bathroom at the end of the hall was an ordeal. Sometimes, as he walked by Tommy's old room, if the door was open, he imagined Tommy sitting at his desk preparing for his next class.

He started skipping classes except for those in his major. Instead of dropping the classes and getting an "incomplete" mark, he let the time lapse to drop classes. Where he could have received no grade or an incomplete instead he got a big, fat F. He was closing doors instead of opening them.

He dropped out of college and returned to his summer job at Learned and Patterson. The big difference being that in summertime, the outdoor job was great for keeping a tan and flirting with girls when they walked or rode their bicycles. In wintertime, it is cold, wet, icy, and just plain miserable; still branches had to be pruned from the power lines to prevent local power outages. The work had to be done.

It was a recurring dream. He was in a sterile room with four doors arranged by the cardinal points: north, south, east, and west. He took all doors one by one, but each door led him into another identical room as the one he had just left. He was going nowhere. He could not get the thought of Tommy's passing out of his mind.

Every day was the same. Get up, go to work, come home, shower, eat supper, and go visit Julie. The monotony was destroying his soul. He identified a heavyweight, like a steel beam in his heart where before it was always light like feathers. He needed more challenges; he needed inspiration. He wished that God made him into someone interesting. It was so easy to forget that there is any joy at all in life. So what was the use of just seeing and feeling things if you could not express them? It was a misfortune, but it was there with him. How was he going to get out of this vicious circle? Was he going to give up and accept the current circumstances, or would he fight for a better life?

He would fight. Marco remembered his dad's words so many years before:

"Son, you'll have the opportunity to take charge of your life. To make your own mistakes and to mend them if you have the moral courage." It was time to take charge of his life.

He missed his Marist friends. Occasionally, he would ride to Poughkeepsie and spend the weekend with them. One Saturday, he saw one of his Spanish professors, Brother Weiss. They sat down for coffee and conversation. Marco did most of the talking, and Brother Weiss listened intently. Just as Marco was ready to say good night,

Brother Weiss asked him if he would be interested in coming back to school and going to Spain with his classmates. Marco nearly fell off his chair. Yes, yes, he would be ecstatic to return to school and go to Spain. Brother Weiss only asked that he study harder, and Marco promised that he would.

He drove home, feeling as if he had just won the lottery. For the second time in his life, a human guardian angel had saved him. This time from a major mistake since he was no longer a boy of thirteen; he was nearly twenty years old.

At last, he fully understood that change comes from within. It was up to him to get up and fight for a better life. It was not his parents, family, girlfriend, friends, the college, Democrats or Republicans, the social environment, or the battle between good and evil. It was up to him to change the pattern of his life for the better. Opportunity was in front of him; he would grab it and never let it go.

CHAPTER 4

All summer long, he worked at his old job, chipping away and learning the tree service business. One summer day, he got terrible news. For the last couple of months, Jimmy, the same Jimmy who missed the prom a couple of years earlier because of sickness, was not well. Jimmy had some sort of cold and was at home healing. It also happened that Jimmy was "going steady" with Julie's best friend, Dina.

They had a lot of double dates that summer, but now as the time for travel to Spain approached, Dina and Julie told Marco that they had bad news. Jimmy did not have some sort of cold; he had cancer and was dying. Jimmy's parents had kept his illness a secret from his friends, but felt that Marco should see Jimmy one last time before going to Spain.

When Marco entered Jimmy's room and saw his friend, he nearly started crying. Jimmy was so emaciated that he resembled a cadaver, his skin white like a sheet of paper. Jimmy was one of his earliest friends when Marco came from Cuba. Marco met Jimmy's mom, dad, and two younger brothers. It was the perfect family. Here he was at the tender age of nineteen, dying from an incurable disease. No doctor and no medicine was available for him to get up from the bed and continue his life journey. All that was missing was time. Time ticked with each heartbeat until that young heart ticked no more, but time kept on ticking as it always had because time is inexorable.

In two years, Marco had lost two dear friends. One to a canoeing accident, and the other to cancer. For the first time in his short life, he thought about his own mortality. Life was a game of chance.

It did not matter whether rich or poor, black or white, young or old. When your time was up, it was up.

Marco had experienced a bit of depression when Tommy passed away. He did not recognize it at the time, but with Jimmy's illness, he was sensing similar symptoms. He knew that he had to fight back or suffer through another lugubrious period.

He also knew that neither Tommy nor Jimmy wanted him to feel guilty about their misfortune. It was all part of life, and life, after all, life was not fair. He knew he had to live. To take risk, step up during tough times, and never ever give up. He had been through different but tough times before. The country of his birth was a Marxist heaven; he came to the United States when only eleven years old with the understanding that he may never see his parents again; he lived in a tenement building, experienced poverty for the first time, and got mocked and ridiculed by "friends." He had built a second world from the ruins of the first one. He was a survivor!

CHAPTER 5

Marco was traveling with the students headed for French universities. Their classes did not start until the mid-September. Flying at thirty-five thousand feet over the Atlantic Ocean on an Air France airliner, some of the students began singing, "Row, row, your boat..." Marco thought this was completely asinine. It was as if he was traveling with a bunch of eight-year-olds instead of twenty-year-old young men and women. He wished he could run and hide, but there was nowhere to go inside the flying tube.

Marco's airliner landed at Orly Airport, Paris. He did not have to attend conversationalist Spanish as his classmates did since he was already a native speaker. His classmates arrived in Madrid three weeks earlier to take the course. Marco spent a couple of days exploring Paris before taking a flight to Madrid.

A couple of his buddies met him at Barajas Airport, Madrid. After collecting his luggage, his buddies took him to meet the Spanish family he would live with during the school year.

It was an old elegant building where his "Spanish family" resided. The exterior walls adorned with beautiful mosaics. The main door located on one of the building's corners. It gave an impression of being swallowed when entering the edifice. A reception area led to a graceful set of stairs and an old-fashioned elevator. A sort of slab door, a panel that slid from left to right. The tiny elevator resembled a birdcage. He was warned that it was only safe when going up. It was not a good idea, he was told by the porter, to ride the elevator down.

His "Spanish" family greeted him at the door. His first impression was that the husband and wife team were really small. They resembled miniature Lego people. He was probably five foot two, and she probably did not crack the five-foot level. He felt like a giant, a skinny giant, but nevertheless, a giant next to the two of them. They turned out to be a wonderfully caring couple. They were probably in their late fifties or early sixties. She looked her age, but he looked much older and in poor health. He smoked a lot.

It was a large apartment. Four bedrooms, a bathroom, a small kitchen with a tiny refrigerator, and a dining room that doubled as a sitting room. Marco's room was fitted with an iron bed cradling an uncomfortably soft mattress, an armoire for his clothes, and a desk with a lamp that produced a lime-yellow color. A window opened to a funnel-like structure, and one could detect indistinguishable conversations emanating from the other apartments. It was a bit strange. The bathroom was efficient, and the toilet paper was rough, almost like fine sandpaper. He got his mom to send him a steady supply of American toilet paper.

The first evening meal was a fiasco. Marco always a picky eater and did not eat fish. The dinner table was tastefully presented, and the family sat for the meal. The room filled with laughter and conversation as Marco was welcomed into the family. The main dish served. Before Marco was a large fish, a complete fish, scales, teeth, and all. The head slightly outside one side of the plate, and the tail also residing outside the other side of the plate. Marco looked at the fish that was staring back at him with his one open eye. He knew that this was an honorific meal. He had experienced the same in Cuba, but he could not make himself dissect the fish like in biology class to get to the meat while that one eye kept gazing at him. He did the best he could and apologized telling them that he did not like fish. They looked at him as if he had instantly grown a second head in complete astonishment. They thought to themselves, *Who does not like fish?* With the kabuki drama over, everyone resumed eating and having a good time. The Mrs.— made Marco a Spanish omelet, the first of many he would eat during the year.

CHAPTER 6

With two and half weeks before the start of the semester, they decided to take a trip and rented two cars. One was a Seat 500, the other a Seat 850, both quite small by American standards. The former with tiny engine of 633–767 CCs, and the latter had a "robust" powerhouse of 843–903 CCs. So Lenny, Mike, Joe, Karen, Liz, Tammy, and Marco piled into the cars and headed out of Madrid to their first destination: Toledo.

Lenny was the brains of the group. He was well-versed in every subject. Of medium built and height, a scruffy beard, dandy mannerism, and an ever-present cigarette dangling from his mouth. Mike was the tallest of the group, at about six foot two. A considerate and hardworking guy, and a smoker. Joe had that tough Brooklyn look. He was missing the tips of a couple of fingers and wanted to be a cop, and he was also a smoker.

Karen was not a Marist student. She attended a school in Massachusetts, but she was part of the group. She had blue cat-like eyes, dark hair, and smooth olive skin, probably from her Italian genes, and she already had a Spanish boyfriend with whom she was terribly in love. Liz carried herself with confidence. Short, dark hair and dark eyes with a pretty smile, wicked smart, and a smoker. Tammy was the fairest of the girls, freckles, and blue eyes, and a terrific person. All in all, it was a great group; the girls and guys stayed in separate hotel room, which was a good idea since it prevented jalousies.

Toledo is a short distance southeast of Madrid. It is a beautiful ancient city where Arabs, Jews, and Christians lived and worked in peace. El Greco made it his home. The Alcazar of Toledo is a stone fortification that dates to the third century.

During the Spanish Civil War, Colonel José Moscardó Ituarte, its commanding officer, held the fortress against overwhelming Spanish Republican forces. During the siege, his son was captured. The Republicans demanded the Alcazar's surrender; in return, his son's life would be spared. Ituarte refused to negotiate. His son was shot and killed, but he never gave up the fortress. Franco's forces liberated Toledo and the fortress following a long siege. After visiting all the sites, El Greco's home, the El Alcázar, local cuisine, and discotheques, the group took off in the cars, next destination, Segovia.

Packed like crayons in a box, they reached Segovia, another majestic and ancient city. There was much to see in the city: the Alcázar of Segovia, center of royal power for Ferdinand and Isabel, the inspiration for Walt Disney's castle on TV; the Roman Aqueduct; the Royal Palace of La Granja; the Segovia Cathedral; and, of course, discotheques. At a restaurant known for its tender roasted piglet, so tender that waiters sliced the meat with a plate, Marco had a déjà vu. As he was looking out a window at the Roman Aqueduct, he had a sensation that he had been in Segovia, although, in this life, he knew it was the first time. He wondered if he had been a Roman Centurion or just a worker assisting in the building of the aqueduct. By the way, the piglet was delicious!

On the way to Salamanca, they made a brief stop by the walled city of Avila. Home to Santa Teresa of Avila where they saw a relic: her finger. In Salamanca, they spent time visiting the university. At the main entrance is the famous façade—the *fachada*. The school legend said that if a student found the frog a top of a skull, then it would be a successful year. They all looked for the frog; they all found it. A successful scholastic year lay ahead of them.

They had wine and cheese at the Plaza Mayor—Salamanca's Main Plaza. Marco was playing pinball when Lenny brought a large dish of onion rings. Marco took one and started chewing and chewing and finally swallowed. He said, "These are really strange onion rings. I can't taste the onions."

"That's because they are not onions. They are fried calamari."

Marco spit out the remaining slivers in his mouth and drank wine, like a sailor, trying to get the taste out of his mouth.

Suddenly, the Tuna—a group of university students in traditional university dress, playing traditional instruments and singing serenades, strolled into the plaza, filling the night air with sweet music. Of course, that night, the group ended in another discotheque. Marco danced to a slow song with Karen. He never knew all the words to a song, but he was singing along anyway when Karen told him to stop because he messing up the song. That was the end of his singing career, for now.

Next stop, Santiago de Compostela. They decided to go Northwest via Portugal. Crossed the border into Portugal, and headed north. For some unknown reason, nighttime arrived early as they drove in a mountainous area; it was a pitch-dark night, no moon, and even the stars were shy that evening. The cars had a difficult time negotiating the hills because of their lack of power. For a while, they thought they may have to sleep in the cars until daylight because the headlights lacked bright luminescence, and it was an unfamiliar and dangerous road. They shifted people around, the lighter folks in the 500, the heavier ones in the 850. It worked. That night, completely exhausted, they parked the cars in a Santiago de Compostela parking lot and tried to go to sleep.

When the first greyness began filtering into the car, they got out and stretched their weary bones. When it was nearly light, they found themselves in front of the primary sight they had come to see—the Cathedral of Santiago de Compostela. The magnificent structure is mainly of Romanesque architecture. It also the burial place of Saint James, one of Jesus's apostles.

As Marco wiped the sleep off his eyes, he noticed a few ragged-looking people carrying a staff and a scallop shell prominently hanging from their necks. Marco, not knowing who these folks were, said, "Man, look at those folks. They look like they been on the road forever. They look dirty and probably smell awful."

Our resident encyclopedia, Lenny, said, "Those are pilgrims. They probably started their journey in southern France and have been on the road for days, if not weeks. They stay in hostels along the way. If the hostels are full, then they sleep outdoors until they finally reached their destination—here, Santiago!

"For over a chiliad, pilgrims have taken to the road on the Camino de Santiago, the Road of Saint James. Of the most popular caminos, the Camino Frances is the best known. It has the best accommodations or infrastructure hospitals, hospices. It passes through monasteries, hermitages, and churches that have a spiritual meaning for many pilgrims. The Camino Ingles, the English Way, led English pilgrims arriving at La Coruña to Santiago. The Camino Portugués, the Portuguese Way, brought pilgrims north to Santiago, and Vía de la Plata, the Silver Way, took pilgrims from the south and middle of the peninsula to join the Camino Frances in the city of Astorga.

"Pilgrims are easily identified by the scallop shell displayed around their necks, backpacks, or hats. According to legend, one of Santiago's early miracles was his salvation of a drowning horseman who resurfaced covered in shells that are abundant in the Galician seashore.

"Non-Catholics, agnostics, atheists, walk side by side with Christians. Each pilgrim has his own reason for taking the way: penance, fertility, in memory of someone dear. In fact, the reasons are as many as there are pilgrims.

"Credentials are distributed through the Church by authorized parishes. Its purpose is to identify the pilgrim that go on foot, bicycle, or horseback. It also has two practical applications: access to the infrastructure of the Camino and to the *Compostela*, the certificate awarded by the Church to the pilgrim after completing the pilgrimage with a religious motive. The *Compostela* is akin to a passport. As a pilgrim progresses in their trek, their *Compostela* is stamped by authorities. Keeping a record as proof of his journey."

The group was in awe of Lenny's knowledge. They felt like they were in the presence of a young sage. He was, in fact, a walking encyclopedia.

After finding a hotel and enjoying a good meal, they got ready to see the sights. The ancient city offered many religious and historical venues: Monte de Gozo, Monastery of San Martiño, Museo del Pueblo Gallego, and, of course, the cathedral. The start of the semester was quickly approaching, so they boarded the uncomfortable cars and headed back to Madrid. It was a terrific expedition in so many ways: culture, folklore, historic, regionally, and most importantly, without knowing it, they had become a tight-knit group.

Throughout the trip, Marco felt right at home with the culture and architecture. Spain colonized Cuba in early sixteenth century and kept it until 1898 when it lost it to the United States following the Spanish-American War of that same year. From one of Spanish professors, he learned that for Spain, Cuba was much more than a colony; it was another Spanish province as if it were in the peninsula.

Spanish and Cuban cuisine are very similar, including the fish dish with scales and eyes. For Marco, the main difference in the spoken language was the accents. Of course, in some parts of Spain, accents varied. Cubans tended to speak fast and to cut word endings. Much of the Spanish spoken on the peninsula was Castellano Castilian—the mother language. He compared the language differences to the way Americans speak English to the way the English speak English. Certainly, you understand each other's variances, although sometimes one has to pay a little more attention to capture the full meaning of what is being said.

The architecture was also extremely familiar to Marco. Marble floors and walls adorned with bronze tiling were familiar. The churches and monuments, elaborate tilework, iron grillwork, cantilevered balconies, narrow cobblestoned streets, covered porches, and arcaded walkways reminded him of Cuba. So far, his time in Spain was like being back in Cuba—minus Fidel.

CHAPTER 7

The metro, a bus, a short walk, forty-five minutes later, Marco arrived at Universidad Complutense de Madrid. He registered for the following courses: western history, eighteenth-century Spanish literature, Spanish folklore, and advanced Spanish composition. The classrooms' designs were old-fashioned. Long tables in a sort of semi-circle pointed the students to the center of the classroom where the professors delivered their lectures. The American and Spanish students shared in the discussions. It was an atmosphere that Marco admired and felt quite comfortable.

There were two sessions, morning and late afternoon. In between sessions, they went back to their Spanish families for *almuerzo* (lunch). It was customary to have wine with the meal and lots of conversation. Lunch came to an end when the *postre* desert was served. Then came another custom that Marco had not practiced since he left Cuba—the siesta!

Then it was time to take the metro and bus back to the universidad. Marco was all in for this very civilized routine. Before he knew it, midterm grades were posted, and he had done well achieving a cumulative score of 3.4 out of a possible 4.0.

Often, after class, the group would get together and go for wine and cheese and talk about the day's events. Marco noticed that the Spanish of the girls in the group was better than the guys. They were picking up on the accent and the nuances of the language. They probably started dreaming in Spanish, which is another sign of language development.

One evening after one of their after-school outings, Marco went home to find an older man making himself comfortable in the room adjacent to his. It was going to be an interesting meeting.

CHAPTER 8

His name was Juan, and he was about thirty years old. A big man, 6 foot 2 inches and 220 pounds. Dark hair covered a big head, a large bushy moustache adorned his upper lip, onyx beady eyes reflected high intelligence, perfect teeth, soft manicured hands with shiny fingernails like a woman's, and a soft body that was a stranger to exercise and manual labor. But a trained sharp mind that attacked an opponent's weakness with facts and rhetoric. He was a true Bolshevik.

During dinner, Juan had prodded Marco about Fidel Castro's revolution and how much better off the Cuban people were under his Marxist regime. Marco was not sure what to make Juan. Was he egging Marco, or did he really mean it? After dinner, Marco adjourned to his room. A short while later, there was a knock on the door. Marco answered it. Juan was standing there and asked if he could come in. They talked about ideas, Marco mostly listening. Juan skillfully discussed labor unions, independent labor, cooked-up wage scales, minimum salaries, living wages, secularism, and higher taxes on the rich.

Marco's brain was adrift as Juan threw statistics and revisionist history at him. His mind had a hundred disorganized thoughts that prevented him from debating Juan toe-to-toe. His only retort at Juan was what he had experienced under Marxism, and that just was not good enough. He needed more knowledge to debate a thoroughly indoctrinated person like Juan. Juan's Marxist knowledge overwhelmed Marco. It was as if he carried a miniature copy of *Das Kapital* in his breast pocket, and Lenin was whispering in his ear all the approved talking points.

Juan was in Madrid preparing to defend his political science PhD dissertation. Day and night, he studied, and Marco was the object whom he practiced his Marxists machinations. His circumlocution was designed to be equivocal in what was at that time a government, an anti-Marxist government, under the strong anti-Marxist hand of Francisco Franco. Marco was glad to see Juan return to Galicia, his home in Northwestern Spain and site of Santiago de Compostela.

As Christmas recess approached, the group made plans to travel to France and Italy. Marco missed Julie and decided to go home to see her. He arrived at Kennedy Airport on a blustery, wet, cold day. The weather resembled the greeting from Julie. She was polite, but that was all that could be said about the reception her received from her. Julie had found a new boyfriend. He was not sure. To make a dreary Christmas recess even sadder, Jimmy finally succumbed to cancer. Marco had lost a girlfriend and a real friend in a two-week period. He looked forward to boarding the plane to Spain.

CHAPTER 9

His first semester was a success with a 3.5 grade point average. He felt confident, pleased that he was not letting down Brother Weiss, and glad that he had spotted the frog on top of the skull on Salamanca University's lavish *fachada* covered with many small sculpture designs. He was on a scholastic roll and was going to maintain the pace.

Marco registered for the Golden Age of Spanish Literature, twentieth-century Spanish literature, Latin American literature, Latin American history, and Western History II. A full schedule, but he was sensing a maturity for learning he did not previously possessed. Additionally, he took up reading Marxist and liberal literature. He knew that to skillfully debate Marxists, he had to learn more about what he considered to be a dubious philosophy. His personal experience living under Marxism was not enough.

Marco made time to read about nineteenth-century Russia, the Russo-Japanese War, Russian Revolution of 1905 and 1917, biographies on Lenin and Stalin, and other issues. He continued his Russian education when he returned to the United States; he never stopped reading he had a lot of catching up to do.

It does not matter what road you follow. All highways lead roundabout to your destiny. He quickly fell into the routine of going to class, meeting with group after school, and studying. Weekends were usually spent at the Prado Museum, exploring the Madrid sights during the day and discos at night. They became regulars at one disco and got to know the disc jockey well, named Mario. Liz and Mario started dating.

One morning, Karen showed up at school in tears. She and her Spanish boyfriend—the one she was madly in love with—broke up. The girls were excellent at consoling Karen. In a short time, Karen was back to her vivacious ways.

Sometimes the group missed the United States and would go to American Embassy's cafeteria. Here they listened Americans going about their routines. They also had the opportunity to eat pizza and drink real Coca-Cola. The pizza was not very good, but they got their longing for the US recharged, at least, for a little while.

CHAPTER 10

Madrid under the Franco regime was one of the safest capital cities in the world. There was little crime. The Guardia Civil ensured the capital's crime free reputation, but there was a cost. Music reminded Marco that they were living under a strict regime. American Pie, by Don McLean was a popular song in America as well as in Spain. The song's lyrics included "the Father, the Son, and the Holy Ghost." These words were muted in Catholic Spain. A reminder to Marco and his friends that free speech was not a guarantee.

Marco and Karen were back at their favorite disco talking, drinking and dancing. As they were dancing, their cheeks slightly brushed. Marco felt a spark, and so must have Karen. They stopped dancing, looked into each other's eyes, then a flame-like passion kiss followed. The two rejected, forlorn colleagues found comfort on each other's arms and were no longer forgotten. A passion flame now burned, but would it last?

They were a couple now, at least until the end of the school year. Karen lived in upstate New York and Marco in Port Chester, close to New York City, but they carried on as a couple anyway. During Easter recess, the two of them traveled to the Gran Canarias where they enjoyed beautiful weather, the beach, and the unusual terrain of the Canary Islands. From Good Friday to Easter Sunday, it seemed that all businesses closed for a time of reflection, penance, and finally a time to rejoice. The Catholic theme of guilt and sorrow was present through those three holy days.

Keren had an old Volkswagen Beetle. At every opportunity, the two of them traveled to see the Spanish sights, landscapes, museums, and, for Karen, to get a better understanding of the culture. They spent a weekend visiting the El Escorial, a residence for Spanish kings, in the town of San Lorenzo de El Escorial, some thirty miles northwest of Madrid. Phillip II built the site that functioned as a monastery, basilica, royal palace, pantheon, and library.

They drove to Granada in southern Spain and explored the Alhambra, a palace and fortress built in AD 889 on the remains of a Roman fortification. In Barcelona, they spent endless hours in Las Ramblas. They boarded the gondola that took them to the Monserrat Monastery that lies just outside the city limits.

On another occasion, they took the road north to León. The main attraction being the gothic cathedral, which was built on the site a previous Roman bath. Most of the cathedral was built between 1205 and 1301. With the stay in León, Marco had visited the land of his great grandparents. His maternal side from Barcelona and the paternal side from León.

The semester was half over. Marco carrying a 3.5 cum through the midterm. He continued reading everything regarding Marxist theory. If Juan came back, he wanted to be better prepared to debate him. It turned out that Juan was back at the apartment. Marco's "Spanish" family congratulated him. He had successfully defended his dissertation. He was now Doctor Juan. There was no debate, for he had just stopped by to thank the family for all the hospitality and was heading home to Galicia. Marco wished him success and was glad to see him go away.

June was quickly approaching and with it the end of the semester. Some were making travel arrangements back to the US while others prepared to spend the summer in Europe traveling.

The semester ended well for Marco. He finished the entire school year with a 3.5 cum. He felt confident and proud that he had not let Brother Weiss down.

The group got together for one last reunion. They went to their favorite restaurant, followed by a walk on the Paseo del Prado. The streets full of men and women going about their business. Cafés redolent of roasting coffee and bakeries creating a mouthwatering aroma of freshly baked bread. In the end, they landed in their favorite disco. Karen and Marco found a quiet corner while the music played and agreed that they would meet again in the states. They embraced, and their lips met.

A day later, Marco said his goodbyes to his family. They said that they would miss him and told them the same. Next thing he knew, the Iberia airliner was landing at Kennedy Airport. It was June 1972, and it was hot.

PART III

CHAPTER 1

Marco's parents moved to a better neighborhood while he was in Spain. They now lived on Washington Street, which was located across from Our Lady of Mercy School and church. The farther up you went on Westchester Avenue, the better the neighborhoods. His family had come a long ways from the tenement on 15 South Main Street.

He could not understand how a person born in the United States who knew the English language and culture and was educated with at least a high school degree failed to provide for his own subsistence without government assistance. His parents had come to the United States in their midforties with none of those advantages and thrived in the American system. To him, this was proof that with steady work, patience, and money saved the capitalist system provided the opportunity for a better way of life. Under Marxism, he knew, his family would still be residing in South Main Street, receiving whatever the government was willing to dole out, which was just enough to get by. Marxism was simply the antithesis of the pursuit of happiness. Instead, its motto should be the pursuit of misery.

That summer, he was back at working at Learned and Patterson and playing in a softball league. He and Julie had moved on. Julie with her new boyfriend, Marco looking for a new girlfriend. He did see Karen a couple of times during the summer, but they lived too far away to have any real relationship.

He continued the practice started in Spain—reading the work of liberal writers such as John Dos Passos, Richard Wright, Joseph Conrad, Arthur Koestler, H. L. Mencken, Louis Fischer, Ignazio Silone, George Orwell, and other terrific thinkers and authors. Their genius was their power of persuasion, their complete mastery of their language. He could not help but be captivated by their ideas, even when he disagreed with many of them.

As his senior year began, Marco was appraising issues with a deeper sense that comes through experience and knowledge. He was still an emotional guy, but now he reflected on what his experiences and serious readings had taught him.

He could not understand why smart educated people easily surrendered to the siren call of Marxism. Why the very same people that gave the benefit of the doubt to Marxist ideas failed to do the same for capitalists ideas? It was all there in black and white—the deceitful practices of Marxism.

Many people have their eyes open, but they do not see. It was as if their minds were sensitive and willing to believe anything that sounded easy. It was these very same people that kept mountebanks well-fed and hence support their deceitful attractiveness. They find it completely impossible to differentiate between what is true and what is false. He thought about the circus leader who said something like there is a sucker born every minute.

For Marco, a Marxist is simply a person suffering from an overwhelming compulsion to believe what is false. They believe, at some point in their lives, that they are Socialists, or at the very least, Progressives, a new term that he had recently discovered. There is no problem taxing the rich and middle class, evangelizing, prohibition of private property, government-run economy, free healthcare and education. False promises designed to win over people ready to be had.

CHAPTER 2

The college years were beginning to be fun. Learning became a priority after Brother Weiss gave him a second chance at success.

One thing he never understood was why so many of his classmates were liberal or leaned to the Left. The human character is infinitely adaptable and infinitely gullible. Often, in the classroom and outside of the classroom, he heard classmates denigrate the American way of life while promoting Marxism as the answer to all world problems.

Is this false teaching what they were taught at home, high school, and now college? Were they ever offered a different point of view? Had they read the likes of Arthur Koestler, Whittaker Chambers, Ignazio Silone, Richard Wright, and others disillusioned by Marxist?

Marxism is inimical to liberty and freedom. The very core of liberty is the realm of the individual—liberty of thought and feeling. It did not only maintain the privacy of the individual over the state but also in the moral authority. By promoting secularism, they remove God from the moral equation. If there is no God, what is there to fear? If there is no after life, there is no one to account to for your earthly sins. Then the state encouraged morally unacceptable actions that otherwise they would not dare even consider.

The Left attempts to express their humanism by opposing capital punishment. Never mind that the people in death row had committed despicable acts of murder. They should be given a second or third chance at rehabilitation. However, the most vulnerable, the unborn, don't even get a first chance at life!

Lately the leading principle among the young has been the 'Left.'" The essential word is 'progressive.' You do not want to be identified as a 'capitalist.' The Left for the last ten to fifteen years has been gaining popularity with the people. They promote slums, unemployment, and condone a cowardly foreign policy. They give the impression that failure and weakness is more delicate and a more noble thing than success and strength. It was a stagnant period led by mediocre leaders that allowed for a fertile ground for Marxist and Progressive recruitment. Redistribution of wealth is the favorite socialist slogan after social justice.

Marco thought: for one man to take something from another to increase his own advantage at the price of another's disadvantage is contrary to everything in nature. It destroys fellowship and trust among men. If any man will steal, belittles, or use violence against another for his very own profit, then, things that are in accordance with nature will be destroyed. Humanity will be shattered into a million pieces. It is a way for leaders to sound magnanimous, caring for the less fortunate, but in reality, it is a way to keep themselves in power. It is not their wealth after all, it is someone else wealth they are giving away—simply—it is stealing!

Now we come to the question of social justice, he pondered. Social justice is not justice. Social justice is very much like redistribution of wealth; it takes from the true owner and gives it to someone else. Justice is justice. It serves all equally. In the end, beware of any modifier before the word justice; whether social, economic, or any future modifier that fits the "Left" cause. It is a political maneuver, a cynical design to get votes.

After all, natural rights are permanent and immutable. Less government means more freedom. The more government regulates, the more respect for the law is destroyed. Hiding behind an opaque veil, Marxism promotes equal justice and living standards for all. This they accomplish by standing on high moral pedestal. Then with a magical microphone and multiple loudspeakers for everyone to see and hear the false message declaring class rejection and equal treatment for all. The Marxist lie perfidiously takes control over the beguiled people.

So the Cuban people thought they had the great liberator, Fidel Castro, the leader that would break the Cuban historic cycle of dictatorships. Instead, Castro declared himself a dictator, no chance of free elections as he had promised while he was in the Sierra Maestra.

Moving forward, he started blaming all the country's ills on the United States. This tactic fell in line with previous Marxist's successful practices. Lenin said, "One must be prepared for every sacrifice, to use if necessary every stratagem, ruse, illegal methods to be determined to conceal the truth for the sole purpose of accomplishing, despite everything, the Communist task."

Like Stalin, Castro thought that the industrial and social programs can be accomplished easier through the agency of an authoritative regime. At last, when he was securely in power, Castro declared that he was Marxist, Leninist, and a Communist. He had lied to the Cuban people, at least, from the time in the Sierra Maestra, if not before. He nationalized all American businesses, cozied up to the USSR, and removed all challengers to his omnipresence in the style of Stalin.

To guarantee his unchallenged leadership, he stealthily removed any possible competitors from the scene. Camilo Cienfuegos, an extremely popular man, died in a mysterious military aircraft crash. His body was never found. Ché Guevara, restless in his administrative responsibilities and disgruntled with Castro, took to revolutions in Congo where he failed miserably. Ironically, he died in Bolivia at the hands of Bolivian Special Forces trained in the United States and coordinated by a Cuban official of the Central Intelligence Agency.

Then there are those that treat human beings not as rational thinking beings in search of his self and his Creator. Instead, they determined human beings are best served by a relatively small cadre of superior men that can guide them as if they were a flock of sheep since they are not smart enough to search for their own well-being.

As if a weak and irresponsible government was one that promoted a negative individualistic social policy. An efficient and responsible government promoted a positive comprehensive social policy.

It logically followed that the great enemy of individual government was a big government or Marxism since its doctrine encroaches upon the innate liberties of the individual. If you call yourself a Marxist, then organized society must, above all, use its powers to establish conditions where the masses possess actual power over liberty. The rights which the people now possess are provided by the society, which he now belongs and not by his Creator.

A true Marxist believer overlooks the 1956 and 1968 Hungarian and Czechoslovakian revolution crushed by Soviet tanks. They promote the Molotov-Ribbentrop Nonaggression Pact of 23 August 1939 as a treaty that insures the growth of the Communist Party. However, for many in the intelligentsia, this was the straw that broke the camel's back. They felt betrayed by the very system they believed was the proper philosophy to prevail over human suffering.

The nonaggression pact signing was too much for the likes of Arthur Koestler and Whittaker Chambers. Koestler was an English writer with socialists' tendencies. During the Spanish Civil War, Koestler furtively supported the Spanish Republicans while writing for a British anti-Franco newspaper. During the length of the civil war, Republicans were backed by the USSR while the nationalists received backing from Germany and Italy. Koestler was captured by the Nationalists, imprisoned, and nearly shot. He was exchanged for a nationalist prisoner held by the Republicans and found himself back in England safe and sound, but now, with extreme doubts regarding the benefits of socialism.

Whittaker Chambers, disappointed with capitalism, as was the case with much of the intelligentsia throughout much of the 1920s and 1930s, saw Marxism as the answer to all the people's ills. For years, Chambers spied for the USSR, providing America's enemy with valued intelligence. He believed in the USSR's path for equality until he felt betrayed by the Molotov-Ribbentrop Pact. He then realized that what the party's leadership was selling was not equality, but its own survival. Like many other fellow party card holders and travelers, he had been tricked.

Ignazio Silone was an Italian liberal writer, a Marxist that lost his tarry faith in that flawed philosophy. As a writer, he sensed the stifling oppression directed from Moscow to prevent freedom of expression and opinion by competing parties. What struck him the most was how exceptional Marxist personalities were unable to provide a fair discussion venue in discussing opinion that conflicted with their own. The rivals, by promoting a different opinion, immediately became traitors. No more discussion, the end.

As an African-American writer, Richard Wright viewed Marxism as a way to break free from the black-and-white American divide to a classless society where everyone is equal. Wright's disillusionment with Marxism reached its peak when he was told that members of the party do not violate the party's authority, but he had the courage to violate the party's authority, and for that, they tried to destroy him as a writer and a person.

Therefore, for Marxists, effective liberty is a function of social conditions at any given time. If you do not know the difference between real liberty and effective liberty, then, they thought, men would be denied constructive comparison. Time is the key to reprogram the people. With total control of government, they had all the time in the world.

The Left-leaning forces, whether foreign or domestic, were fighting against capitalism. They saw it as tyranny, and if they overthrew it, then Marxism would take its rightful place. But leftist governments, everywhere, in cities, states, and countries invariably disappoint their supporters.

It is safer to overlook the plain facts and pretend they can put everything right by redistributing the nation's wealth. They forget that a nation, as well as individuals, do not get wealthy by sitting on their laurels. It is the hardworking, innovative, sacrificing, saving people, and the solid family structure that make a country rich, stable, and prosperous.

Even if government squeezes the rich out of existence by "paying their fair share," it would not be enough to support a Marxist regime. In time, the government coffers would empty since no one is producing, but only taking. It is as if Marxist's refusal to work is honorable. No doubt about it, Marxists want what capitalists have but not by sacrifice and hard work.

There is no perfect adaptation of man to society, yet Socialist and Progressives try to put everyone in the same social box. Even though humanity is a complex and not just one piece of large pie, is a concept that free people accept. Every attempt to simplify this truth, every effort to reduce everything and everyone to the same common denominator is, and always be, pernicious and dangerous.

Socialism is the belief that all of society can be altered by turning people into society altering machines. The "Left" takes advantage of man's suffering by preaching that suffering is the road to salvation. Their goal appears to be one where unrefined taste and want of nicety are advantageous instead of the reverse. The socialist definition man: he was born, he suffered, and he died. There is another pattern, the most obvious, perfect, and beautiful, in which a man was born, grew to manhood, married, produced children, worked for his daily bread, and died.

Reality is that other men, with no more advantage than the next, succeeded, and others, with many more, fail. Some people are weak and others strong. The physical and emotional needs of one are not the same as others. Some are beautiful while others are ugly. Those with greater talents and work ethics will receive greater rewards. Some are born into families that provide all for success and yet fail, while others are born into dysfunctional families, prosper. The unsuccessful will always continue to envy the successful. There are not two people alike. The bottom line is that we are all different human beings with feelings and not exactly the same pitiless machines that socialist attempt to produce.

On one hand, Marxists harangue about the plight of the less fortunate, the downtrodden. They feel their pain and resort to improving their dismal lives by attempting to provide for them: an apartment in a tenement building, a stipend to buy food, and receive basics health care.

On the other hand, Marxist elite never wear hand-me-down clothes. They are dressed in the finest garments, and live in comfortable homes. They may mingle with masses during a protest, but never ever live in the same poor neighborhood.

Marxism corrals the masses in a circle of despair and misery. They do not care that human beings must have dreams, hope, and drive. Power is what Marxists seek and take by any means.

Some people think that someone who committed a robbery is strong. If you analyze it from the thief's point of view, he senses that the entire world is against him, and there is no escaping his misery.

Marxist thinking is similar to the thief's reasoning. They believe in making government bigger, which means more taxes, really stealing, is what keeps Marxist government growing. The result is decreased buying leverage for the wage earner. It also means more government power that takes away from the liberty of all citizens. Now everyone is less free, and governing socialists have more authority. Instead of high tide that raise all boats, Marxist low tide drains the harbor and with it all boats go aground making everyone equally miserable.

Picture a philosophy that its goal is misery. What type of person would create such a malignant path? It would be a person of unmatched venom, selfishness, and resentful of his peer's joy. Willing to destroy friendships, wisdom, happiness—all to satisfy his thirst for retribution for his miserable life.

Someone else's happiness makes his life even more wretched, for he cannot dare to hope that someone be happy while he is miserable. He would rather take down the entire system that offers a path for the pursuit of happiness to one that only provides a road to bare existence and all just for revenge. This is a philosophy that is not content in suffering alone; it is only satisfied when all are equally dissatisfied, living in abhorrent conditions with no way out. It destroys all hope, only to satisfy its own cheerless existence. This philosophy is Marxism, a close relative of Communism.

CHAPTER 3

The school year seemed to fly by like a rocket ship between the schoolwork and the people he was meeting. Marco was back at Marist for his senior year, but fifteen credits behind his classmates. He would not graduate with his classmates in May 1973. He took more history courses, advanced Spanish literature, Latin American history, and conversational Spanish for new freshmen, helping Brother Weiss. He had a full schedule and was truly enjoying the educational atmosphere.

Louisa was one of the students he was helping with conversational Spanish. She was absolutely adorable. Thin, but extremely shapely, smart, and with a terrific sense of humor, she was fun to be around. She drove a mustard colored jeep. Marco thought that was so darn cool, and it seemed that she always wore Roper boots. She had a special way of talking that mesmerized Marco; she seemed to speak from the side of her mouth as she was letting you in on a special secret. Nothing romantic ever developed between the two. Months later, Marco felt that Louisa was the one that got away.

The fall semester ended, and Marco kept a 3.4 cum. He went home for the Christmas break and ran into Julie. She had finished her first semester at Tulane University. They spent a little time together, and it seemed like old days for a little while. She was still seeing the same boyfriend, but Marco got the impression that the fire was not burning as brightly as before. They decided to keep in touch as they both went back to college.

He met another cute girl, a Spanish major that was taking one of the advanced classes with him. Her name was Lisa. She had big, expressive blue eyes and dark, wavy hair. Smart, fearless, and with a Bronx accent, she was fun to be around. Marco thought to himself that if you dared her to jump out of airplane without a parachute and rendezvous in midair with another person that would hand her a chute, she would not hesitate and go for it. It was only a matter of time before they started dating. They saw each other all that summer, then she went to Spain for her junior year, just like Marco had done a couple of years before.

Marco's final semester at Marist was finished with a flurry of success. Julie asked him to apply to Tulane to pursue his MA. On a whim, Marco took the Graduate Records Examination (GRE), History Specialty GRE and Spanish Specialty GRE. To his surprise—no, to his amazement—he did well in the standard GRE, very good in the history and outstanding in the Spanish GRE.

He completed his Tulane application, mailed it, and again, to his amazement, he was accepted. Marco remembered seeing a bumper sticker that said, "The Harder You Work, The Luckier You Get." He was a believer in the saying, for he did not give up when things were looking bleak.

That summer Marco registered at Iona College to finish the BA requirements and was back at Learned and Patterson working at what now seemed like his regular job. In August 1973, Marco completed the requirements for his bachelor of arts degree. He delayed starting the master's program at Tulane until January 1974, for he was looking forward to visiting Lisa during her Christmas break in Spain and needed to make money for the trip.

He spent a couple of weeks with her. They went to Toledo, El Escorial, and Segovia. They also explored El Prado and other museums, the Royal Palace, and many historic sites.

Throughout the summer, Marco continued his professional readings in an attempt to understand the liberal's romance with Marxism. This time, he focused on Progressives, the political term he knew nothing about and that he had heard discussed in school.

There is nothing new under the sun, after reading about Progressivism. What there is, however, is dusted-off ideas that with a successful propaganda campaign gains momentum. This is accomplished by using the popular terms of the times, but the intended goal is the same as the original idea.

After living with all the Castro deceptions, manipulation, threats, and lies, Marco had his own theory as to why Americans can be swayed by covert propaganda and misinformation.

Americans are easily deceived because it is in their nature to root for the underdog. Unlike Marco and the millions of other immigrants who left their chaotic countries in search of a better life in the United States, Americans have not experienced turmoil that turns friends and family into lethal enemies since the Civil War. That terrible period was only remembered in books and recently, even that, had been revised to fit the Progressive view. Basically, the average American is politically naïve and, therefore, easily susceptible to propaganda, tendentious polls, and bias media that spread misinformation every single day.

It turned out that the term *Progressive* was an idea originally constructed by a German philosopher Georg Hegel, which became the foundation for Karl Marx's civil society and his book *Das Kapital*. What is it about Germany that they produce some of the greatest philosophers, politicians, and scientist while at the same time creating horrible philosophers, politicians, and scientists?

Someone always seems to take up a bad idea and make it their own. Usually, this is done by academics in their laboratory, the classrooms, and not by the hard knocks of real life. John Dewey, Frank Goodnow, Herbert Croly, and Woodrow Wilson were such academics. They made their pedagogical credentials by expounding Hegel's idea that eventually became known as Progressive.

Of course, as it always seems to be the case, second or third-rate thinkers see this an opportunity to advance their own lives in the political, academic, media, and entertainment fronts. Under the guise of caring for all people, they push policies that weakens the individual and promote the role of the state. If all humans were programmed robots, these policies would work, but humans are not programmed robots. Each person is an individual with different aspirations.

When power becomes the ultimate goal, freedom must be shackled. They all agreed that government should play a larger role in the life of the citizens. That the state takes precedence over the rights of the individual, technological advances contributed to the formation of social organization, and that modern education should be responsible for the thoughts of the coming generation, that private ownership was a burden on the state, and that the state should manage private industry and free trade. In a nutshell, Progressivism is a euphemism for Marxism.

CHAPTER 4

With goodbyes said and well wishes pronounced by his family, Marco hit the road for New Orleans, the Firebird packed to the gills with his gear. He figured it would take him a couple of days to reach his destination: Tulane University. He reported to a main office and was given a key to his room in one of the dormitories. A little while later, Marco received a call from his sponsor, a student working on his PhD, who introduced him to a couple of Cuban girls that had completed their MA's first year in Spanish Literature, the same program that Marco had signed on to pursue. They had a few days before the beginning of classes, so they did much socializing while getting a good familiarization of the campus.

Spent long hours in downtown New Orleans taking in all the sights: Jackson Square, Café Dumont, and way too much time in the surroundings of Bourbon Street. New Orleans was beautiful, exotic, and a big temptation.

Julie arrived for her sophomore year. They spent time together and even had a romantic encounter once or twice. They had a good time, but Marco knew that what they had once shared was over. Their relationship was friendly, but it was never the same.

Marco sat in an old classroom surrounded by his fellow aspirants. He looked at the old-fashioned ceiling with solid beams distributing and carrying the roof's weight. Marco felt exactly like one of the beams—carrying someone else's weight. He was there for someone else and not for himself. Looking at the future did not seem appealing. He was not looking forward to being a high school Spanish teacher. If he did become a teacher, it would be at a college or university. This meant working towards a PhD after the completion of his MA. He counted the years of more education. The idea of sitting in a classroom and doing research for a dissertation did not have any appealing stimulus. He would be nearly thirty years-old or older before he accomplished that goal. For the next few days, he thought about alternatives. One morning, he awoke knowing exactly what he really wanted to do.

CHAPTER 5

As a kid in Cuba, he grew up with the sounds, sights, and smell of aircraft. His dad, a master sergeant in Batista's air force, would take him to Columbia air base, which was next to his home. In fact, from his front porch, Marco saw Douglass C-46s transport airplanes. He loved the sound of planes landing and taking off. On a few occasions, his dad took him inside a B-26. One time, a pilot gave him a tour of the light bomber. He was mesmerized by the lights, gages, and the smell so unique to airplanes.

Marco decided to join the navy and become an aviator. He dropped out of school in time to get his tuition, room, and board money back. Then he called home. His mother had a fit; she could not believe what he had done. She saw him safely in a classroom and someday as a professor at a university. She handed the phone to his dad. "What did you do? What are you going to do now?"

He told him his story and that he was going to join the navy to be an aviator. His father said, "Good choice."

With the Firebird packed, Marco returned to Port Chester. A few days later, he drove to Long Island where the navy's officer recruiting center was located. He took the written test and eye test. Passed them both and started the recruitment paperwork. It was going to take a little time before he would know if he was accepted or rejected. In the meantime, the recruiter gave him practice problem pamphlets on algebra, vectors, liquids, and physics.

A few weeks passed, and he received the good news. He was accepted into the program and had a VIP invitation to Pensacola to experience what the aviation program for himself. He flew Delta Airlines to Pensacola and berthed in one of the battalion barracks. Along with a group of guys from all over the United States, they witnessed what was expected of them if they decided to become officers in the United States Navy.

They were introduced to marine drill instructors charged with transforming them from civilians to military men. They were shown the basic aviation curriculum, the classrooms, the place of workshop, the gyms, swimming pool, obstacle and cross-country courses; in short, they were allowed to ask as many questions as they wanted and to see all that they wanted. It was going to be a challenging sixteen weeks, and if you were good enough, you would be commissioned an ensign in the United States Navy. Marco was ready for the challenge.

Back home, he started getting in shape for what he knew was going to be tough physical demands on his body once in Pensacola. He studied the practice academic problem the recruiter had provided. He knew this was going to be the toughest part of the program for him because math and science had never been his strong suit.

CHAPTER 6

Time to get physically and mentally ready. He had an interim report date of mid-October 1974. A background investigation was still in process. So he ran three or four miles and worked on his practice problems everyday.

Lisa lived in Long Island. He would take the two-hour car ride to see her fairly often. They were becoming a couple, but he was still seeing Julie occasionally. Julie would often call him after she had a fight with her boyfriend, or maybe she was just getting tired of him. In any event, Marco's love life was doing just fine that summer.

His background investigation was successfully completed. His report day was still mid-October. Now all he needed was a set of orders from the navy personnel. In the meantime, he kept studying, running, and seeing a couple of nice girls. He enjoyed his last civilian days; he knew that what lay ahead in Pensacola was no picnic, but hard physical and mental work.

In his short life, Marco had experience dictatorships in Cuba and Spain and a republic form of government in the United States. He knew that the opportunities the United Sates offered easily outclassed what dictatorships offered.

All he had to do was look at what his parents had accomplished in thirteen years in America. They came with nothing from Cuba, only the clothes on their back. They had improved their standard of living by leaps and bounds. They rented an apartment in a middle-class neighborhood, owned two cars, and paid for their son's private school education. This was a real-life example of the American dream. Marco knew that America was special. No other country in the world would have offered an opportunity to get out of poverty and thrive so soon.

It was now time to give back to the country that he loved and respected. It was time to defend and protect the Constitution of the United States, and for him, there was no better way than join the US Armed Forces.

A package arrived. It was his set of orders along with a packet of information about reporting to Pensacola, Florida. At last, Marco was ready to embark in his new life. An American way life!

FIGMO!

ABOUT THE AUTHOR

Rafael Polo was born in Cuba. He came to the United States in 1961 as part of the Peter Pan Project and grew up in New York. He became a United States citizen in 1970. He was naval officer and retired with the rank of commander after a twenty-year career. He then went to work in the intelligence community and retired in 2010. This is his first novel.

CPSIA information can be obtained
at www.ICGtesting.com
Printed in the USA
FSHW022231080821
83909FS

9 781644 714744